2056

SCOTT GELLER

Contents

-1-

"Amber Matlock?" The woman at the desk finally calls my name, signifying that it's my turn to go for my examination.

"Okay honey," my mom looks me straight in the eyes. "You know what we've talked about."

"Yes mom," I nod my head.

I do know what we've talked about. This examination is to judge my health and fitness, to see if my name will be put in the Manitoba bowl of names of fifteen year old girls. My mother wants me to completely fail the fitness part. She had to keep me healthy though, otherwise my five year old brother, Ty and I will be taken away, my parents deemed unfit. But I'm not failing the fitness part. I know that a lot of girls purposely do, but not me. I've been training for it. I want my name to be drawn for Manitoba. I want to become a GovChild, as we call them, and find out what happens.

So I raise my head, and walk confidently to the counter.

The woman ushers me behind the counter and takes my weight and height. Then she walks me into the exam room.

It is a large room. One side of the room is like a normal doctor's office, while the other side is an exercise room, and a much nicer one than the community centre has. In the center of the room, there is a desk, with a computer. Sitting at the desk is the doctor that will be performing my examination.

"Hello Amber. My name is Doctor Ross," she says.

"Hi," I say shyly.

"So Amber," she says. "We're going to start with the medical exam, which should be just like any other regular doctor's appointment you've ever had. Then we will move on to the physical exam, which I will explain to you when we get to it."

The medical exam goes quickly, and is slightly awkward, like any other exam. Then we move on to the second half, which I breeze through.

"Alright Amber. We're done here. Let me just total up your score." She pauses to look at her computer. "Okay. Amber, you've passed both tests with flying colours. Looks like your name is going into the bowl."

She gives me a sympathetic look, but inside I'm jumping for joy.

"Okay," I say, keeping a blank expression on my face.

I feel slightly bad, because I know my mom will be devastated if I get chosen, but this is what I want. I know my mom wishes that I had been born a year before or after the year I was born, because then I would be safe. Ty, my little brother is safe, because he will be fourteen in an even year, the year that they'll draw fifteen year old girls. And I'm glad of that, because Ty is small, and weak, and probably wouldn't do well if his name was drawn. He is much more dependent on our parents. Me on the other hand, I want to escape the curfews, and patrols of my current life.

I am quiet as my mom and I walk home. We are not supposed to share the results of our exams with anyone, and I can't give anything away.

The drawings will happen in two days, and if I am drawn, my mother will know that I passed, if I'm not, she'll never know how I did.

All of a sudden, the city's alert siren goes off.

"Citizens of Winnipeg!" A voice booms. "Please return to your homes immediately. There is an important broadcast from the Government of Canada that will come on as soon as you turn on your television or radio. Please wait until all of your family members are at home to watch this broadcast."

The announcement stops, and my mother and I quicken our pace.

The announcement is repeated several more times throughout our walk home.

My mother and I enter our house, and join Ty and my father on the couch. My father turns on the television.

"Greetings citizens of Canada!" The prime minister's cheerful voice calls out. "I would like to inform you that some changes have been made to the drawing system, for the ADCCG, the Annual Draw of Children for the Canadian Government. This year, all the children who passed their exams will be standing right in front of the stage, instead of with their families. The children who did not pass will be watching with their families. One name will be drawn, but anyone who passed may volunteer to go in the drawn child's place. Everything else will continue as normal, the drawn child will still get to say their goodbyes, and so forth. And to any girl whose name is in the bowl this year, good luck to you! If your name is in the bowl, you may let your family know. Thank you."

The screen fades to black, and my father turns off the TV.

"Amber?" Ty asks, "Is your name in the bowl?"

"Yeah, bud, it is."

"Oh! Honey!" My mother cries. "No! Not my baby's name in the bowl! Oh love!" She wraps her arms around me and cries.

Once Ty and I are in bed, I hear my parent's hushed voices.

"David, what will we do if she's drawn?! I couldn't bear to go through it again!"

"Shhh Penelope. It's okay."

"No! Honey, it's not okay! I worked with her; I told her how she could fail the examination! I cannot do this again!" My mother says in distress.

Do it again? What does she mean? I'm their firstborn child.

"Penelope," my dad says softly. I lean my ear against the vent in my room so I can hear better. "Maybe this is what she wants."

"No! That's not possible! How could she want it? She would become government property! How could anyone want that?!"

"Dear, if she doesn't want it, I'm sure she'll talk someone into volunteering for her. But if she does go, she'll do well doing whatever the GovChildren do. She's a tough cookie, Amber is. Don't stress it too much."

"But David, how can you say this? How can be so calm, when we might be losing another child?"

"I would be sad to see Amber go, Penelope. Just like I was sad when-"

The air conditioning comes on, and I can't hear what my dad says.

Slowly, I slip into a deep sleep, with no thoughts of the draw in my head at all.

"Amber! You're needed downstairs!" My father calls.

I push my sheets off of me and jump out of bed. I pull on grey sweats and a hoodie, and run downstairs.

I pass Ty, who smiles at me and blinks his dark brown eyes, which are the mirror image of mine.

I follow the sound of my parents talking to the front door.

"Good morning Amber!" My mother says cheerfully.

"Morning Mom."

I try to be as happy as I can around her, knowing the amount of pain I will put her through tomorrow.

"Amber, this officer is here because-"

Wait. An officer? What? I look to the door, and what do you know, there's a government officer there.

"-your mother thought that there might have been some error in your fitness test, as she didn't believe that you would be able to pass it," my father continues.

"Oh?" I say, surprised.

Wow Mom, I think. Way to make me sound weak.

"So I called ADCCG, and they sent an official to have you do the test again, with your father and I watching," my mother says.

"Okay. So I just have to redo the fitness test?" I ask.

"Yes," the official says gruffly, looking at me critically.

I am suddenly aware of my knotted, brown hair and the bags under my eyes.

"Honey, run upstairs and get ready, and then we'll go," my mom says.

"Okay. Is Ty coming too?"

"Yes."

Once get back into my bedroom, I shut the door and I rifle through drawers to find some athletic clothing. I settle on a black Dryfit shirt, and blue Adidas shorts. I lace my shoes and head back downstairs, where my mother waits with a bowl of oatmeal, which I actually hate.

She looks at me sympathetically.

"I know it's tiring, but I'm doing this for you Amber," she says.

Oh, if only she knew. But based on the conversation I overheard last night, I think my dad has figured it out. If I wanted to, I could have failed the fitness test, but I didn't.

I choke down the disgusting oatmeal, and then my whole family follows the ADCCG official to their complex, and takes us to a high tech gym.

+++

An hour later, I'm purely exhausted.

The official tells me that once again, I have passed the fitness test, and that my name will be in the bowl.

My mother's face goes sheet white, and it's almost enough to make me regret my decision. But nothing can me regret it.

I think back to five years ago.

It's the day of the drawing. One boy from each of the thirteen provinces will become government property today, and there's nothing that their parents can do about it. They all signed the contract when their child was born. If they didn't, their child would already belong to the government. I get ready, in nicer clothes than usual. Normally, my family does not attend the drawing; we normally just watch it on television. But today we are going, because my best friend's brother, Mitchel, is in the bowl. Tasha asked me to come to support her. Her brother is like her best friend. Even with the four year age gap, nothing could come between those two. But the government did-taking Mitchel away, and changing Tasha's life for the worse.

Last year, up in the North West Territories, the boy drawn had a speech impairment, and could not speak. But he was drawn, and taken by the government.

I just have to know what happens to these teenagers. I feel like it's my goal in life.

My family walks home together, everyone but Ty silent.

When you're five, you don't understand all of this. Ty knows the basic concept of the ADCCG, because children learn that in kindergarten. But he hasn't fully grasped the concept that I could be gone forever by tomorrow.

"Amber!" Ty exclaims, grabbing onto my leg, "Piggyback ride! Please Amber!"

"Okay," I exhale.

I'm exhausted, but I love my baby brother too much to say no.

I bend down and he climbs onto my back. It's a good thing that he's a scrawny little kid; otherwise I think this would kill me.

"Faster Amber! Faster! Faster!" Ty shrieks with excitement.

"Sorry buddy. Your big sister is slow," I say panting, "You might have to carry me home bud."

Ty makes a cute face of surprise and doubt.

"But you're too big for me to carry, Amber!"

"It's okay bud," I say as I put him down, "I was just kidding."

Ty laughs.

"I love you Amber."

And at that moment, I don't know how I'll ever leave.

+++

After a hot shower, I get ready to go to Tasha's house for the afternoon. I get dressed in jeans and a t-shirt; knowing that Tasha will be wearing something similar, and not really caring if I don't look like a celebrity.

"Amber! I've missed you!"

"I know! It feels like we haven't seen each other for a really long time!" I say.

"Want to go on the balcony?" Tasha asks.

Tasha lives in a huge house. Her parents are really rich, and she's always had anything a girl could want, including looks. Tasha has vibrant green eyes, and strawberry blonde hair, and at the age of fifteen has already had four boyfriends. But she's never flaunted any of it, even though she could. Tasha is one of the most humble and down to earth girls I know, and the best bestfriend I could ask for.

We get up to the second story balcony, which is our special place.

"So, did you pass?" Tasha asks me.

"Yeah. You?"

"Yes. I'm terrified for the draw tomorrow."

"Don't be. If it isn't my name called, I'll be volunteering. I'm probably the only girl in Manitoba who wants to go."

"Amber, you're so weird. But I love you anyway."

Then reality hits Tasha.

"But ohmygosh! I'm going to miss you so much Amber! I'll be best friend-less!"

"Tasha," I hug her tight.

"Please don't make me cry today Tasha. We'll have time for that tomorrow, when they give us time to say goodbye. But today, I just want to have fun with you. Please?"

"Yes Amber. Today, we'll do whatever you want."

"Okay," I pause and think, "We should go get ice cream, and then go to the park."

"Okay," Tasha giggles, "Let's do it."

+++

I really enjoyed my evening with my best friend, but now, as I lay in bed trying to sleep, I start to think of all the things I will miss. But I'm going to do it.

+++

I am locked up in a cell with no way out. "Help me!" I scream, but there is no one here to hear me. I cannot understand why I wanted to do this. I am being starved to death, and locked in a cage, all in the name of government science. This can't be legal! There is no possible way for this to be legal. But they are the government, they make their own rules. Oh why! I should be having sleepovers with Tasha, attending school and watching Ty grow up! Why does the ADCCG exist? What is the point of this? I scream even louder.

"Amber?"

"What?" I groan.

"Amber, honey, are you okay?"

"Mom? What just happened?"

"I don't know Amber. You were screaming the house down in your sleep."

It all comes flooding back to me. My nightmare about the ADC-CG. But I can't let that get to me. I can't let fear get in the way. I know that I am a strong person, and I will do this.

"I'm okay mom. It was just a nightmare. I'll go back to sleep now."

"Okay Amber. Goodnight. I love you."

+++

"AMBER!" Ty shouts, jumping on top of me, quickly waking me from a deep sleep.

"Hey Bud," I say, smiling.

"Amber, get up!" My mom calls from down the hall, "You know what today is."

"Yes Mom."

Ty starts bouncing on my legs. I pick him up and hold the squirming five year old above me.

"Amber!" Ty shrieks "Put me down!"

I laugh, "Never!"

"Amber and Ty! That's enough! You need to get ready, now!"

Whoops.

"I'm sorry Mom!"

Ty looks at me sadly.

"Okay buddy," I say, "time to get ready."

I go and take a shower, and when I go back to my room I find that my mother has laid out a beautiful dress for me to wear.

The dress is a plum colour. The top is like a short sleeved blouse, and around the waist there is a bow, and the bottom is just a plain skirt. I love it.

I put the dress on, and then my mother comes into my room.

"Oh Amber! You look gorgeous!"

"I love this dress so much! Where did you get it?"

"It's a special dress that I've had for a long time. Maybe one day I'll tell you the story."

I want to tell her to tell me the story now, because I may not be here tomorrow, but instead I just nod my head.

My mom sits me down and does my hair into a fancy french-fish-tail-twist.

"Do you want makeup Amber?"

"Ehh," I contemplate it, "no thanks."

I'm becoming government property, not going to prom. I'm fancy enough thank you.

But of course I don't say any of this. I want my memories of this day to be sweet ones, not sour moments because I was grumpy, or rude.

"Here Amber," my mother says, interrupting my thoughts. "Put these on."

She hands me a pair of silver flats, which go perfectly with my dress.

"Thanks you," I breathe.

Soon enough, we are all ready, and we head to the city square. It is packed. I have to leave and go stand with the other fifteen year old girls, so first I kiss each member of my family, and then go stand beside Tasha.

"My boyfriend is here," she whispers to me.

"Cool. You look really nice."

And she does. Tasha's strawberry blonde hair is up in a perfect ballerina bun, and her dress is a flowy white one that makes her look like an angel.

Then the ceremony starts. A representative from the ADCCG gives a speech about how important all of this is. Then she goes over the new drawing procedures, and starts the draw.

"Okay!" She shouts into the mic.

"And the lucky girl is..."

She over exaggeratedly fishes around in the bowl, and comes up with a slip of paper.

"Amber Matlock!"

I hear a shriek, one that could only belong to my mother.

"Amber, please come up to the stage."

I push my way through the crowd, and walk up onto the stage.

"And here she is! Amber Matlock, Manitoba's ADCCG girl of 2056! Let's all give her a big hand!"

And the crowd does clap politely for me, but most of them just feel sorry for me. And the other girls are just glad that it's me instead of them.

The woman says a few more things, and then hurries me off the stage.

She looks me in the eye.

"Okay honey. In case you missed it, I'm Sandra. You are doing a very good job of staying calm. I'll tell you, we've had much more emotional people over the years."

"I'm generally a pretty calm person," I tell Sandra.

"Awesome. Right now, you're going to get a chance to say your goodbyes. Anyone who wants to say goodbye is waiting in a different room. After you've seen everyone, I'll be back in here."

And with that Sandra leaves the room.

In come some of my friends from school. Beth, Maddy, Joanne, and Ashlyn. But not Tasha.

The girls all hug me, and cry. I hug back, and say that I'll miss them. They wish me the best, and go on their way.

Then my old neighbour comes in, and the frail old lady hugs me, and says that I've always been a good person. I'm not quite sure what she means bye that, but I thank her and say goodbye.

Then it's Tasha's turn. She enters the room crying, even though she knew this was coming.

"Amber!"

I hold her tight, and we cry.

Ten minutes later, there is a knock on the door, and a guard tells us that Tasha's time with me is up.

"Bye Tasha! I love you!"

Then, my family comes in. Ty jumps into my lap. I hug him tight, and give him a kiss.

He is whimpering, "what if I have to go? I don't want to go, Amber!"

"Hush. It's okay Ty. You'll never have to go bud. I promise!"

"Okay," he whimpers, his tearful face staring up at mine.

Then I look over to my mother, who is crying buckets.

"Oh Amber!" she says, "My poor baby Amber!"

"It's okay mom," I say, "I'm tough."

She nods, and my father smiles.

"I love you guys so much. All I ask is that you don't forget me."

"Amber," my father starts.

"Amber we'll never forget you!" My mother shrieks.

Then, the knock on the door come.

Time is up.

I release Ty from my lap, and hug and kiss them all one last time.

"Goodbye!" I say sadly.

Sandra enters the room again, and explains to me that we are going to board a plane that will take us to ADCCG headquarters, which is a secret location.

The two of us board the plane, and I ask her why I can't bring anything with me.

"The ADCCG has everything you could possibly need."

Okay. Then hopefully it won't be like my dream.

Then Sandra explains to me that tonight I will meet the other 12 girls that were drawn today. We will be staying in a large hotel room together, and they will take us to the ADCCG tomorrow.

After that, Sandra pulls out a book and starts to read. I fall asleep.

Sandra shakes me awake.

"Amber! It's time to meet the girls!"

I groggily follow her off the plane, into a black SUV, and to a hotel.

I zone out through a little introductory speech, and just catch that we're going around introducing ourselves by name and province.

The first girl starts.

"Umm, I'm Sadie, I'm from British Columbia."

She is pale, with incredibly long brown hair, and beautiful, but scary grey eyes.

"I'm Zoe, from Ontario," she says, sticking her nose in the air. Of course. Ontario can be a snotty province, being home to Canada's capital and all. She flips her hair and sighs.

The next few girls all blend together, Aria from Alberta, Erica from Newfoundland, who for all the money in the world, looks like a duck. No joke, she has like permanent duck face going on. And there's Marie from Quebec.

The next girl that stands out is Tess, from Nova Scotia. She is really short, and has very pale skin, dark hair, and pretty blue eyes. She looks like someone I could actually be friends with.

Then Beatrice from Saskatchewan, Dawn from Prince Edward Island, Maggie from New Brunswick, Ana from Nunavut, Paige from the North West Territories, and Jenna, from the Yukon Territory.

After we're done, ADCCG reps take us to our hotel rooms.

As we walk, I say to Sandra, "I hope you don't expect me to remember all of those!"

She just laughs.

"Goodnight Amber!"

I've already forgotten most names. I remember Zoe, the snotty one, Duckface, Tess, and...

That's it.

I sleep.

M y personal Sandra alarm clock wakes me up.

"Amber! Get up! It's time for breakfast, and then we're going to the ADCCG headquarters!"

"Urggghhh."

I drag myself out of bed, and look for my favourite sweats and hoodie.

But then I realize that I don't have any of that with me.

"What are you looking for Amber?" Sandra asks.

"Clothes," I tell her.

"Oh," she says.

She passes me a pair of skinny jeans and a faded yellow hoodie.

This is good, I think, this is what I normally wear.

I quickly get dressed, and follow Sandra down the hotel hall, into a room set up just for us.

Sandra talks to some of the other girl's reps. She comes back with three other girls, and they lead us to a table.

"Introduce yourselves girls, and then go grab some food," she gestures to the extravagant buffet.

I look at the other girls. Duckface is here, and I don't know who the other two are.

"I'm Erica," Duckface says.

"Cool! I'm Maggie! I'm from New Brunswick!"

Woohoo! I think, sarcastically, That's just so exciting!

"I'm Paige."

"Wait, you're from the North West Territories, right?"

Paige nods, and Maggie continues.

"That's so cool! I've never known anyone from up north before! What's your name?"

"Me? Oh, I'm Manitoba Amber."

"Oh wow! I've heard so many good things about Manitoba!"

Does she ever shut up?

"Does she ever shut up?" Paige hisses in my ear.

"Doesn't look like it."

Duckface speaks up.

"Let's go get some food. I'm hungry."

At the buffet table, I grab a plate and get a waffle, with strawberries and whip cream, and I grab some orange juice. Breakfast of champions!

Just after we get back to our table, a woman makes an announcement.

"Hello girls. I'm Mrs Attary, from the ADCCG, and I'm in charge of welcoming you. After we finish up here, we're going to be taking you to headquarters, where I'll explain a few more things. That's about all for now, enjoy your breakfast, and we'll be on our way shortly."

After breakfast, we all pile into a big bus with tinted windows, and drive to what I'm assuming is the ADCCG headquarters.

When we get there, we are escorted off the bus, and into a tunnel.

All of the adults leave us, and then a scary looking bodyguard guys comes and stands in front of us.

"Is there anyone that doesn't want to be here?!" he bellows. "Because at the moment, you have two choices: fulfill your purpose here, or die!" He pauses for dramatic effect. It works. "Is there anyone unwilling to fulfill their purpose?" He looks around. We are all terrified.

"Good. Let's continue."

He turns and continues down the tunnel, unaware that he just terrified thirteen fifteen year old girls, or that he just did a complete personality change.

When we get to the end of the tunnel, we climb up a ladder, and enter a large entry hall type thing. There is a big crest on the wall, which I assume symbolizes the ADCCG.

"Okay girls listen up!"

Mrs Attary claps her hands.

"Today, you are going to get settled in. We'll match you up with someone whose been here a while, and they'll show you around for the next few days. Also, one thing to note, often, instead of being called by name you will be called your province, and then 56. For example, Manitoba 56, please step forward."

I step forward.

"Good," Mrs Attary praises, "now follow me."

We go through a door, and into a hallway lined with doors, and then reach an area with couches.

"Girls, this is the female dormitory common room."

There are about thirteen girls sitting on the couches, who I'm assuming are the ones that we'll be paired up with. I recognize one girl, who was the Manitoba draw from two years ago.

"Girls, these are the girls that you'll be paired up with. They are seventeen years old, drawn in '54. They will be your mentors for the next while."

She pauses.

"Okay, here are the pairs. Tess, Nova Scotia 56, with Marigold, Nunavut 54."

It goes on and on, until she calls out Amber, Manitoba 56, with Lee, British Columbia 54.

I step forward, and so does a petite girl, with jet black hair, and clear, olive skin. Her eyes are a deep brown, and she is stunning.

We stand beside each other, and the last pair, Duckface and the P. E. I. 54 girl are paired.

"Okay. 56 girls, I'm going to show you to your dorms, and then it will be lunch time, which you will eat with your partner."

We walk down the hall, and Mrs Attary starts to write on a white board.

Dorm a: Sadie/Dawn b:Zoe/Marie/Paigec:Erica/Ariad:Ana/Jennae:Beatrice/Maggief:Tess/Amber

Mrs Attary tells us to go find out dorms, and get to know our dorm mate, and that lunch will be at 1:30.

+++

"So, you're Amber, correct?"

"Yeah, from Manitoba, you're Tess, where are you from?"

"I'm from Nova Scotia."

We spend the next little while getting to know each other. I lucked out in the roommate scheme of things. Tess is awesome. We go out to the couches together and meet our mentors.

Her mentor, Marigold, and my mentor, Lee, are roommates and best friends.

+++

After lunch, we are given time to meet other ADCCG people, including the boys.

"Let's go boy shopping!" Tess jokes, with a glint in her eye.

I laugh.

I thought Tess was kidding, but evidently not, as when we get to the large common room, Tess goes straight to a guy and starts flirting with him.

I'll admit it, some of these guys aren't totally unattractive, but this isn't really my scene.

I take a seat on the couch, and scan the room for Paige, or Lee, or someone else I might know.

Just as I give up hope, a guy who looks to be about my age walks up to my couch.

"Hey," he says, "You one of the new girls? You look lonely."

"Yeah."

"I'm Daniel, what's your name?"

"I'm Amber," I say shyly.

"Nice to meet you Amber. Is it okay if I take a seat here?"

I nod. Daniel's politeness is a little unnerving, but he seems nice.

We keep the small talk going, but eventually it burns out, like a forgotten candle when all the wax has melted.

Daniel and I just sit on the couch silently, grateful for the company. At least, I am.

A few minutes later, Tess comes over, a guy following her wake. I like my outgoing roommate.

"Amber! This is Oliver. I just met him. Who's that?"

"I'm Daniel. Are you Amber's roommate?"

"I am indeed," Tess says cheerfully. "The name's Tess."

"Nice to meet you Tess. It just so happens that Oliver and I are also roommates."

"Oh! Cool!"

Oliver and I just watch this exchange. I almost feel like I am unwanted, but I don't think I am.

Soon, Daniel and Tess have moved on to talking about Nova Scotia. They're both Maritimers.

+++

The rest of the day is gloriously uneventful.

Tess and I lie in our beds in the room we now share, and talk. We talk about our provinces, families, lots of things. The only thing I refuse to say is that I wanted to become and ADCCG girl.

+++

-5-

I knock on the door of my house.

"OPEN UP!" I shout, with a loaded gun in my hand.

My father comes to the door, cowering behind it as he opens it.

I lift my gun.

"You are being evicted by the ADCCG. Comply, or my gun does more than just look scary." I say, my voice even.

"Amber?" My mother cautiously questions from behind my father.

I put my finger on the trigger.

"Allow us to search your house. You are being evicted by the AD-CCG." I state levelly for the second time.

"David, just let them in," my mother insists.

In a lower voice, she asks, "Is that Amb-"

My father's hand flies to cover her mouth.

"Penelope!" He hisses.

Things have drastically changed in Winnipeg. It began a crime-ridden city, and is now being "repossessed" by the ADCCG.

"Agent AM," my supervisor says from behind me.

"Yes?"

"Shoot!"

I aim my gun, squeeze my eyes shut, and pull the trigger.

The screaming is so loud.

"Amber! Amber! Quiet!"

"Huh?" I mutter groggily.

Tess looks at me.

"Amber, you were screaming so loud! You could have awakened the dead! You must have been having a nightmare."

Oh.

It all comes rushing back to me. The dream. Shooting my father. Yes, that's why I was screaming.

"Yeah..." I mutter.

"You good?" Tess asks, sounding legitimately concerned.

"Yeah." I say, more confidently this time.

I shake off the dream.

"I'll be fine," I tell Tess.

"Okay, good. I was worried about you."

"Thanks."

There is a knock on our door.

"Manitoba and Nova Scotia 56?"

Tess an I mirror each other's puzzled looks.

"Uhh," I say.

"I think that's us."

"Okay."

"Yes?" Tess asks whoever is at the door.

"It's me, Sandra!"

I groan, and Tess looks confused.

"My ADCCG rep person," I mutter.

Tess gives me a look of sympathy and understanding. I open the door.

"Hi Amber! How are you doing?" Sandra asks, incredibly chirpily.

"I'm fine thanks," I say, but I'm thinking Oh my gosh just get on with what you want. Jeez woman.

"Well Amber, I just thought I'd come see how you're doing," Sandra looks like she has something more to say, but instead says, "Girls, don't forget that breakfast is in twenty minutes."

Tess and I look at each other after the door closes behind Sandra.

"Okay then," Tess says.

"I guess we should get ready for breakfast?" I suggest.

Tess nods.

Clothes have been put into the wardrobes in our rooms, just generic stuff. I pull out an athletic grey hoodie with neon green drawstrings, and black tights. I'm going for comfort, not style.

Breakfast is just boring, everyday breakfast food. Nothing like what they served us yesterday.

"Look Amber! There's Oliver and Daniel! Want to go sit with them?"

"I guess if they're okay with it. You're into Oliver aren't you?" I ask.

Tess blushes but says, "Maybe."

Tess goes to get some oatmeal, but I skip it. The texture of oatmeal disgusts me.

I'm standing in one place, looking around the cafeteria like a weirdo, when someone bumps into me. My tray goes flying, and I'm covered in cold juice.

"Ahh!" a high, feminine voice shrieks, "You did not just do that!"

I turn around.

"Umm," I say. It's Zoe, that awful Ontarian girl.

"Whoa, what happened?" Two more girls join the crowd.

"This girl," Zoe starts, "she had the nerve to push me over and spill my drink.

Zoe's two lackeys nod in agreement. But the other two can see the lies. Zoe is perfectly fine, but my tray is on the ground, and I'm covered in disgustingly pulpy orange juice.

"Yeah, she totally just like shoved Zoe over."

"Totally right Maggie. It was like, complete madness."

"Oh I know,"

"Beatrice, Maggie!" Zoe barks, "Come back to my room with me!"

The three spin on their heels and exit, looking like a scene from a movie. They look like the beautiful popular ones, even though everyone is wearing a similar hoodie/tights outfit.

"Are you okay?"

"Yeah," I mutter.

"I'm Sadie by the way, from BC, and this is Dawn, from PEI."

"Nice to meet you. I'm Amber."

I remember Sadie now. She was the first one to introduce herself that night, with the long brown hair and amazing grey eyes.

Dawn seems very soft spoken, but both girls seem nice.

Dawn has short, blonde hair, and eyes somewhere between blue and green.

"Amber! What happened?"

Tess has now arrived at the scene of the crime.

"Zoe bumped into me, spilled juice all over me, and blamed it on me." I state levelly.

"Ugh. I hate her already. How come none of the adults came over here?"

I shrug.

Dawn speaks up.

"There aren't any adults in here."

I look around and see that she's right. It's just ADCCG kids.

"Okay," Tess says, "Let's go sit."

I look to Sadie and Dawn.

"You coming?"

They look at each other, and Sadie nods.

"Oh," I say remembering that I should introduce them to Tess, "by the way, this is Tess, my roommate. Tess, this is Dawn and Sadie."

Then I see Paige, sitting all alone.

"Paige! Come with us!"

Paige's face brightens, and the others introduce themselves.

We get to the table that Oliver and Daniel are sitting at, with three other guys.

"Can we sit here?" Tess asks.

"Yeah sure," Daniel says.

There are five empty chairs. Tess takes the one beside Oliver. I end up between one of the guys I don't know, and Sadie.

The guys introduce themselves to us. The other three are Tristan, Ethyn, and Dave.

We eat our breakfast and chat, but it's not awkward at all. Sadie, Tess, Daniel, Ethyn and Dave are huge chatter boxes, so Paige, Dawn, Oliver, Tristan and I are free to just listen in and eat.

All of a sudden, the cafeteria gets very quiet, very quickly.

I look around to see why.

Then I notice Mrs Attary striding into the cafeteria.

"Good morning children," she says, "I trust that you are all enjoying your breakfast. Today is the first full day for our new 56 girls. Please make sure to welcome our thirteen newcomers as you were welcomed. 54 girls, you are mentors, please do your job appropriately. Thank you. You may continue your day as normal. The bell will ring in five minutes."

And Mrs Attary is gone.

"What?" Tess asks, "No orientation or anything?"

"Nope," Dave says, "They just throw you into your new life."

"That's so stupid," Paige states. "Everything about this place is."

"We've all been through it," Tristan says, the first words he's said all morning.

"We'll help you," Daniel offers.

And with that, my first day begins.

+6+

I mportant info in authors note!

The bell rings, signifying that breakfast is over. Daniel, Oliver, Tristan, Ethyn and Dave jump out of their seats.

"Crap," Dave says, "We're going to be late!"

"Late for what?" Tess huffs, clearly annoyed that we are being kept completely in the dark here. I know how she feels, I feel the same way.

"Class, you dumb nuts!" Daniel says, with a near shouting tone evident in his voice.

"Well we don't know! It's our first day, and you offered to help us!" Tess yells. Sometimes she's a little too outspoken.

"And we will," Tristan says quietly. I'm learning that it's not that he's super shy, he's just a man of few words. He says what needs to be said, and nothing more.

Ethyn, Daniel and Oliver start to leave, putting their trays away as they go. Tess, Paige, Dawn, Sadie and I continue to stand by Dave and Tristan, confused.

"Well," Dave starts.

"I was assuming we'd be able to pair up," Tristan says.

"But, they ditched. So, we'll do it ourselves," Dave says, finishing Tristan's sentence.

Tristan nods.

Dave cracks his knuckles. "Okay. Basically, the 55 boys and the 56 girls have classes together, because we're all fifteen now, so we'd be in the same grade anyway. The 26 of us-"

"-25," Tristan harshly cuts in.

Dave gets a sick look on his face, but nods and continues. "All follow the same schedule. We take some normal classes, and some weird ones," Dave pauses and looks at Tristan. "Anything else I missed?"

Tristan replies, "Nope. But we'd better get to class before we're in even more trouble."

"Yeah," Dave agrees. "Let me explain why we're late. Girls, no matter how crazy what I end up saying is, just agree with me. I don't have to tell you, Tristan, cause you already know."

We dump our trays, and exit the cafeteria. Dave and Tristan lead us down a long hallway, with doors on either sides.

"So last year you guys took classes alone?" I ask.

Dave nods.

"Just 13, uh or 12 of you?" Tess confirms.

Another curt nod from Dave.

"What happened to the 13th kid?" Tess asks, being her nosy self.

If looks could kill, Tess would be dead. The glare Dave gives her is scaring me, and I'm not on the receiving end of it.

"Shut up or leave."

Tess shuts up, and we walk briskly down the hallway to the very last door on the left.

Dave knocks and opens up the door. Inside, there are 18 fifteen year olds staring at us. And Mrs Attary.

"Ah," Mrs Attary starts, "You've decide to grace us with your presence." Her voice is dripping with sarcasm.

"I can explain," Dave says.

He'd better be good at this sweet talking.

"Basically, we ended up getting breakfast for the kids in detention. There were some forgotten trays labeled, and we just wanted to help out and deliver them. The students were very happy to receive their breakfast."

"Tristan?" Mrs Attary asks, wanting to confirm the story.

He nods.

"Mrs Attary," Daniel starts. "I saw them do it. They invited me too, but I decided to come straight to class."

"Very well. Continue class as normal."

Mrs Attary turns on her heel and leaves.

"Whose the teacher?" I whisper to Dave.

"No one. We just follow the instructions on the smart board."

"Okay..." Paige says, sounding unsure.

The seven of us take the seven empty desks that are scattered around the room.

I end up in the one beside Ethyn.

Everyone is looking at the screen.

Year 56. Welcome to your first day of ADCCG classes. The year 55s will always be with you, and you will catch on quickly.

Today, your first class (this one) will be short. 55s, please explain a normal day to the 56s. The bell will go in 20 minutes.

"Okay," a guy stands up. "I'm Zach. Basically a normal day starts like this. We always come to this classroom. It's like our homeroom. The screen will tell us where to go. Sometimes we'll stay here and do something like math, history, science or English. Whatever we need for that class will be in the desks. Other times the screen will tell us to go somewhere else. The other classes are..."

Zach keeps talking, but I tune him out. Someone can tell me all the important stuff. Clearly, this Zach kid is the resident nerd in the group. I look to the screen, where the message from before has faded off. Now, new words are appearing.

55, 56. When the bell rings please head to your next class-in the downstairs gym.

Gym. I can handle gym. All the boys have zoned out, like me. I don't blame them. They know this already, what's the point of listening to nerd boy reexplain it to them? I wonder who explained everything to them.

"So, I hope that makes sense. Any questions?" Nerd boy finally concluded his speech.

"Uhh," Duckface starts.

I zone out again, not caring to hear this. I look around the classroom. All of us girls are wearing some combination of black tights and grey hoodies that were put in our wardrobes. I notice that the boys are all wearing different clothes. How did they get different clothes?

Rrrrrrrrrrrrrrrrrrrrrr

Everyone scrambles out of their seats. I guess that lovely sound is "the bell."

I catch up with the group I ate with this morning.

"Dave, how did all of you guys get different clothes?"

"All of us have an "account," and we earn points by getting good grades, and doing extra jobs. Then you go to one of the ADCCG approved computers in the student tech lab, and order different clothes using your points."

"Okay. See, that's actually useful information, unlike what nerd boy was telling us."

Dave laughs. "Yeah, Zach's a bit of a nerd."

"Just a bit, eh?"

Dave laughs. "Yep. Just a little nerdy."

+++

Gym class at ADCCG is weird. It must be one of the "weird" classes that Dave told us about earlier.

Though I guess it is a bit more like a normal school class, in the way that we actually have a teacher. But this is more like a military boot camp.

"Get down for 50 push-ups! Now!"

We all get down, some struggling more than others.

"If you think this is hard," the boot camp teacher starts, "Then the rest of this class will be torture. This is just warmup!"

Most of the class, save for a select few, groans loudly. I stay silent. I don't love push-ups, nor am I very good at them, but I'm a fairly sporty girl. Then next part of class might be better.

"Okay class!" The gym teacher claps his hands. "Now, give me three laps, and then walk one."

This is easy. I like running. Well, sometimes. But I want to run right now.

I run hard, my feet pounding on the ground. A guy I don't know and I finish first, walking a lap together. I'm sure I've never met the guy, but he looks so familiar.

He matches my stride. "I'm Cody."

"Amber," I say. It's not that I don't want to talk, I'm just still a little winded.

"Nice to meet you Amber. Where are ya from?"

I've caught my breath now. "I'm from Manitoba."

"Oh cool! So am I!" Cody tells me.

I snap my fingers. "I knew you looked familiar!"

"Yeah. Did you live in Winnipeg?" Cody asks me.

"Yeah."

"Okay, that's why I don't recognize you. I grew up in Lac du Bonnet."

"Cool. I don't know where that is, but cool," I say.

"It's a small town, close to the Ontario border, on the Winnipeg River. It's in cottage country."

"Sounds nice."

"Yeah. I loved it there," he says with a small smile on his face.

"Amber!" Sadie calls from across the gym. "Come here!"

"Coming!" I call back. To Cody, I say, "Nice meeting you. See you around."

"See ya, my fellow Manitoban."

I head back to where Sadie and everyone else I've been hanging out with is.

"Was that Cody?" Ethyn asks.

"Yeah. Is that a problem?"

"Sort of," Daniel says.

"He's an arse," Ethyn states.

"He's Manitoban," I add, almost pleading.

"Don't go near him," Dave says sternly.

Tristan adds his thoughts. "Amber, it's for your own good."

"Why?" I ask.

"Do you really just expect her to go along with it when you guys are providing nothing to back up your reasoning?" Tess cuts in, before my question is answered.

"Guys!" Dawn calls out. "Calm down."

"Class!" The gym teacher interrupts our argument. "Now, we're going to go outside, and do some archery."

+++

Finally, it's lunch. The ten of us take a table together, with trays of lasagna.

"Okay. Cut the crap. What's so bad about Cody that means Amber can't hang out with him?" Tess goes straight to the point.

"Well," Oliver starts, looking at the boys.

Tristan, Dave and Ethyn all turn to Daniel.

"Okay. I guess I'll start with Alex. Alex was my originally assigned roommate. He was from Saskatchewan. Alex was a really cool dude, and my best friend here. Oliver and Dave were in the triple dorm at that point, with Jared-"

Dave interrupts Daniel. "He's a di-"

"Dave! Shut it!" Daniel interrupts. "So Cody started bugging Alex. A lot. About anything he could. Cody did anything to bring Alex down. All because of Lee, who is a girl from 54-"

"She's my mentor," I cut in.

"Oh. Wow. Well Cody did this all because Cody had a crush on Lee, but Lee liked Alex, not him. The bullying eventually got to be so bad that Alex killed himself. I lost my bestfriend, and Lee lost her boyfriend. The two of us were devastated, but the ADCCG didn't really care. Lee and I became closer because of what happened. She's a really great person, Amber. So then they took Oliver out of the triple dorm, and put him with me."

"And left me with Jared," Dave adds.

"Yes Dave," Daniel sighs. "So Cody pushed Alex to suicide, which is why we don't want you to hang out with him Amber. He's a crappy person and you're an amazing person. The only thing you have in common with him is your province," Daniel finishes.

The table is silent.

"I understand now. Thanks for trying to protect me guys." I say, breaking the incredibly awkward silence.

"No problem." Oliver says.

+++

-7-

W e finish eating our lunch in silence.

"Okay. We need to lighten up. Do something fun," Daniel says. I can tell he wants to stop thinking about Alex.

"I have an idea," Dave says. He turns to the guys to run the idea by them.

"Okay. Truth or dare party tonight!" Daniel announces.

"Our dorm," Oliver adds.

"Okay," Tess agrees, looking excited.

"Wait," Paige says. "We don't know how to get to the boys dorms."

"We'll come get you," Ethyn says.

"Or," Dave says loudly, then whispers to the guys. But Dave sucks at whispering, because we hear every word he says.

"We could invite Lee and Marigold and some of their 54 friends, and a few 53 guys. Then the 54 girls could help these girls find their way."

"Nah," Tristan says. "Lets keep it to just fifteen year olds this time. Plus, what kind of mentor helps their, like, uh, little person, or mentoree, or what ever you call it, sneak out at night?"

"A good one?" Dave suggests, making everyone laugh.

Oliver speaks up. "Girls, just be ready in the girls lounge at five to midnight."

"Eleven fifty-five," Sadie says. "Got it."

When curfew rolls around, Tess and I are under our blankets, with our normal clothes on. Paige will have the hardest time sneaking out, because she's in a dorm with Zoe and Marie. And they aren't invited.

Tess and I exit out room just fine, and meet Dawn and Sadie in the girls lounge.

"Where's Paige?" I whisper.

"I don't know," Sadie says, "I guess trying to get out without Zoe and Marie noticing?"

"Probably," Tess agrees.

We wait a few more minutes.

"What dorm is Paige in?" Dawn asks.

I bite my lip. "I don't know."

"Dorm b," Tess says. "I think."

Sadie looks to Tess. "Let's go. You two wait here."

Dawn intervenes. "No. You two are major chatter boxes. Amber and I are quieter. You guys wait here for the boys."

Tess nods. "Okay."

Dawn and I head down the hall.

"I wonder why the triple room isn't room a?"

I'd never thought about that. "I don't know," I whisper back.

We get to dorm b and look at each other. I gesture for Dawn to go ahead and push the door open.

"No, no. You go ahead," Dawn whispers, smiling.

I shake my head.

But before our little argument is resolved, the door opens, and Paige creeps out of her dorm, bumping into me.

She lets out a little shriek. "Amber! I didn't see you!"

I laugh. "We were coming to get you. Sadie and Tess are in the lounge."

Paige nods, and we stealthily head back to the lounge, where the boys are waiting with Tess and Sadie.

"Okay," Daniel says. "We were just explaining to these two that our way of getting back to the boys dorm isn't the nicest, but it works."

Dawn and Paige, and I have mirroring looks of worry and confusion on our faces.

Dave speaks up. "It's through the heating ducts."

Okay. That's not too terrible.

"Let's go."

Oliver holds the vent cover, and Dave climbs in first. It's a decent size to crawl through, about the size of a pillow.

We follow Dave, with Oliver going last, putting the vent cover on behind him.

We crawl out of the vent and into a lounge that looks exactly the same as ours. But it must be the boys lounge.

"K, follow me," Daniel says. "We're going to my dorm."

Which is also Oliver's, if I remember correctly.

"Here are the rules of our truth or dare parties," Dave says. "We have to stay in the room, or Tristan and Ethyn's, which is next door. My room is on the other side. Jared's in their, but don't worry, he's not waking up anytime soon-"

"Dave what did you do?" Sadie asks.

"Sleeping pill. It's all good. Anyway, we still have to relatively quiet. That's about it."

The others guys nod in agreement.

"Alright let's go." Tristan says.

We all sit down in a circle-ish thing on the floor.

"I'm staring, cause it's my room," Oliver announces.

"What? It's my room too!" Daniel protests.

"Okay. Daniel, truth or dare?"

"Ugh. Oliver I hate you. Um, dare."

"Hmm," Oliver says evilly. "I dare you to tell us-"

"Dude!" Ethyn interrupts. "That's for a truth!"

"No it's not, dumb arse! I said I DARE you to tell us! It's a dare!"

Ethyn throws his hands up in the air. "I give up!"

"Finally," Oliver says. "Okay Daniel. I dare you to tell us which girl in this room you would want to kiss."

Daniel smiles. "Amber."

Oh jeez. I turn red, and hide my face in my hands. Why me?

"My turn." Daniel says. "Tess, truth or dare?"

"Dare." She says. I knew she'd choose dare.

Daniel has an evil glint in his eyes. "I dare you to kiss Sadie for 10 seconds."

Sadie screeches. "Please! No!"

"Oh gosh," Tess says. "Are there chickens, or passes?"

Daniel smiles. "Nope."

"What if I don't want to be included in this dare? Sorry Tess." Sadie pleads.

"Okay. Tess, I dare you to kiss a girl for 10 seconds."

"Not it!" I scream.

Paige follows.

Dawn and Sadie both scream "Not it" at the exact same time.

Daniel considers this. "Okay. I dare you to kiss me for 10 seconds."

"Ohh, Daniel, looking for some lovin'?" Tristan jokingly asks.

Daniel turns red.

I am so confused. He just said he would kiss me, and now he wants Tess to kiss him. Wait, why do I even care? Do I have a crush on Daniel? What the heck? I'm turning into a crazy weirdo teenage girl!

"Amber? You alive? Truth or dare?" Tess asks me.

Oh. I guess the kiss has already happened. "Umm, truth."

"What is something no one knows about you?"

That I wanted to come here.

Crap. Did I just say that?

Everyone is looking at me expectantly, so I guess not.

"Um, I have a little brother."

"You already told me that Amber." Tess says.

Oh. "My mom made me redo the ADCCG fitness test, because I passed it."

"What?" Tristan asks.

"She didn't want me to pass it. So she had me redo it."

"And you passed again." Tess confirms.

"Yeah," I say uncertainly. "Dave. Truth or dare?"

"Truth."

"What do you miss most about your home?"

"My girlfriend. Sadie, truth or dare?"

"Dare. This so called party is getting boring."

"Okay. I dare you to lick Tristan's foot."

"Eww!" Paige and I chorus.

"Ick ick ick ick! Why, Dave?"

"Cause I felt evil," Dave says, smiling. He grabs Tristan's ankle, and pulls the sock off of his foot. Dave holds out Tristan's foot. "Here you go Sadie." The sickening sweet evil smile is still there.

Sadie makes a disgusted face. "Fine."

She does the dare.

"Eww! Where's the water?"

Ethyn throws a plastic water bottle at her, which she catches smoothly and begins to chug.

"Chug! Chug! Chug!" Oliver chants.

We laugh. The rest of the night goes pretty quickly. Pretty soon it's 4:24.

"Okay," Tristan says. "Amber, tomorrow, at breakfast, I dare you to beg Zoe to be in her posse."

"Okay," I say. "And now. I dare you boys to take us back to our dorms. Isn't breakfast in two and a half hours?"

"Yup," Dave says.

Ethyn says, "Let's go."

Tess and I put pyjamas on, and fall asleep almost immediately.

When I wake up, Tess is already up. She looks at me and starts laughing.

"What?"

"I just can't wait to see Zoe's face this morning."

Oh yeah. The dare. Right.

+8+

+ ++ Tess laughs again. "Amber! Your face!" She chokes out between laughs.

"I think you would be similar if you were about to get murdered by Zoe!"

"Oh quit being a baby."

I glare at her.

"You know you love me," Tess taunts.

I pull on light grey sweats and an orange shirt.

"Tess, is your shirt a different colour?"

"It's navy. Why?"

"Because my hair looks absolutely awful with orange. Can we trade?"

"No," Tess says. "Navy's my favourite colour. I hate orange. You'll survive."

Gee thanks Tess.

I pull on my awful orange shirt.

"Ready?" Tess asks.

"Two seconds."

I pull my auburn hair into a high ponytail and then separate the strands in half. I start fishtailing it.

"Okay, let's go."

"You're not going to finish doing that?" Tess asks.

"I'll braid as we walk."

By the time we reach the cafeteria, my ponytail is in a tight fishtail braid.

"Holy crap Amber! You're so good at that!" Tess exclaims, seeing my finished braid.

I see Zoe standing with Maggie and Beatrice in the lunch line. "I guess this is my time." I tell Tess.

"Good luck! Don't die!"

"Thanks," I say sarcastically.

I approach Zoe and her posse.

"Oh. It's you." The face that Zoe considers to be so attractive twists into a nasty snarl.

"Yep," I say, super chipper. "It's me!"

"Want do you want from us?" Maggie asks. "Can't you see were busy?"

Doing what?

"Well Zoe, I just wanted to tell you how much I admire you. I thought I'd walk right up to you and tell you just how much I've always admired you."

The cafeteria is silent. All eyes are on me. I go down on my knees.

"I thought I'd tell you just how much I've always admired you, and then sit right beside you at your table."

Someone laughs. I continue.

"So I want to know. Zoe, can I be in your posse?"

Zoe scoffs. The whole cafeteria is laughing now.

"Well?"

Zoe bursts into laughter. "You? You think I would hang out with you?!"

"Ohhhh!" Someone shouts.

"Burn!" Another voice adds.

"But Zoe!" I say. "You love me!"

The three are in hysterics now. My table has started clapping and whistling.

"I'm so hurt!" I exclaim, pretending to be close to tears.

"Zoe!" Dave shouts. "Such a cold heart!"

Zoe's face changes. You can tell she has her eye on Dave. But he said the thing he misses most from his home is his girlfriend. He said girlfriend, so that must mean they didn't break up. Wow. That's trust. Sucks for Zoe.

I walk back to my table, and find that someone got me a tray of breakfast. Oatmeal, to be exact. Just my luck. Oh well. At least I have food.

Everyone is laughing and talking about my performance, but I am quiet. I choke down my oatmeal and sit quietly.

The bell rings and we all get up. I follow the boys. I remember that our classroom is the last door on the left. If only I knew how to get to the hallway.

We take seats in the classroom and wait for a message on the board.

'55 and '56,Today, your first class is English. You must complete the book you find in your desk, The House of the Scorpion, in the next month, and hand in a report. Please start reading.When the bell rings, a new message will appear. Read the message. Five minutes later, the bell will ring again. Please proceed as directed.

I reach into my desk and pull out The House of the Scorpion by Nancy Farmer. I've already read the book, but it's a favourite of mine.

I open the book and am transported to the land of Áztlan and young Matteo Alacrán.

+++

It seems like only minutes later when the bell rings, interrupting my happy reading.

'55 and '56,For the rest of the day, you will be with your mentors. Your mentors are waiting for you in the cafeteria, each with a schedule for the two of you. Enjoy your time with your mentors.

We all wait for the bell so we can go to the cafeteria.

Rrrrrrrrrrrrrrrrrrrr

Ah, the lovely bell. I follow the crowd to the cafeteria. Once there, I look for Lee.

When I finally spot Lee in the crowd, I walk towards her.

"Hey Amber," she says.

"Hi."

After a long awkward pause, I say, "So, what are we doing?"

"Oh! Yeah. Oh I'm so sorry!" She apologizes profusely. "Sorry, I'm a bit shy around new people."

You don't say. "It's fine."

"Uh, we're going to do some sort of teamwork thing at the pool."

"There's a pool here?" I ask in terror and disbelief.

"There's everything here, Amber."

"Wow"

"Okay, are you ready?"

"Uh, y-yeah." We don't have bathing suits. Maybe we won't be going in the water.

"Let's go."

I follow Lee out of the cafeteria and through the maze of hallways and staircases.

"How do you guys navigate this place so easily?" I ask Lee.

"Have you not had a tour?"

"No."

"Okay. You need one. Meet me in the girls common room during after diner free time. I'll show you around."

"Thanks Lee."

"Okay, we're here. The girls change room is this way."

"Oh." Dang it. I guess we are swimming.

There are generic one piece swimsuits laid out across the bench.

"We aren't the only ones doing this?" I ask.

"Probably not," Lee tells me.

I pick out a suit that looks to be about my size, and slowly, apprehensively, get changed.

"Are you okay?" Lee asks.

"Umm. Not really."

"What's wrong? Girl troubles?"

"No no, not that. I'm terrified of water."

"Oh," Lee says. "You'll be okay."

Duckface and her mentor walk in.

Lee looks me in the eye. "I'll be with you the whole time," she says reassuringly.

"Thanks," I whisper.

We walk out of the change room to the pool.

Already out there are Cody and his mentor, nerdboy and his mentor, and Lee and I.

There is also a guy standing alone by a life guard chair.

"Do I have everyone here?" The dude asks.

"I don't know," Lee says. "Who's everyone?"

"Thanks for that helpful comment Lee. Everyone is Cody and Paul, Zach and Tyler, Amber and Lee and Erica and Angelica."

"Well, considering that there are two sets of guys here, and you know that I'm Lee, not Angelica, I think you can figure out who's missing, Evan."

"Sass queen!" I tease.

Lee scoffs. "We're friends."

Duckface and her mentor, Angelica, come out onto the pool deck.

"Okay! Now that everyone's here, let's get started! My name is Evan, I'm 21, drawn in '49. We're going to do a variety of teamwork challenges today. Is there anyone here who can't swim? I'm not a lifeguard."

Lee looks at me. "I can swim," I whisper to her, "I'm just scared of water, and not very good at it."

Lee nods.

Evan claps his hands. "Our first activity starts with those boats over there. They are a cross between a canoe, and the flat kind of kayak."

I look over. They are long, with two places to kneel, but flat, and easily tipable.

"Go grab paddles and get in a kayak!" Evan instructs.

Lee grabs two kayak paddles and we head to the boats.

"I'll climb in first, and then you can get in, K?"

"Okay."

Lee slowly gets in the boat.

"I did this a lot at home," she tells me. "Just stay low and keep your weight centred."

I nod. I step into the boat and kneel on my spot in the back. I see Duckface get in, and immediately tip the boat. She and Angelica come up coughing and try to climb back into the boat. Once they get in, everyone is ready.

"Listen up everyone!" Evan yells. "We're going to race to the other side of the pool, okay? Ready? On your marks! Get set! GO!"

Lee starts paddling hard, alternating sides. I copy her motions.

"Good job Amber! You're doing great!" Lee encourages me. I don't respond, focused on paddling.

I see that Zach and Tyler and Erica and Angelica are both in the water, trying to climb back in. All we have to worry about are Cody and Paul, who are right behind us, and catching up. As they pull up beside us, Cody flips us using his paddle. I make the mistake of screaming, and get a mouthful of chlorinated water. I close my stinging eyes, and trying to swim to the surface. But I'm so disoriented that I don't know which way is up. I paddle frantically and finally break though the surface, just as my lungs were about to give up. I cough and sputter.

"Amber, are you okay?" Lee asks me, sounding quite concerned.

"Yeah. But I think my fear of water may have grown." And my hatred for Cody.

+++

Dinner is over, and I'm waiting for Lee in the common room. Free time started five minutes ago, but she isn't here yet.

I sit on a couch and wait for what seems like hours.

I check the clock for the thousandth time. Two minutes left before curfew. Guess she's not coming.

I get up and walk to my dorm. Just as I arrive at me door, Lee walks up to me.

"Amber, I'm so sorry! It's just-"

"Don't worry, I get it, you're older, have more important things to do than show me around. Whatever."

"Amber, that's not it at all. I was talking to Cody about what he did to you."

"Oh Lee. You didn't have to do that! That must have been hard."

"So you've heard?"

"Yeah. The guys told me because I was going to become friends with him. We're from the same province."

"Oh. Well, it's basically curfew, so goodnight Amber. I'll give you a tour another night, promise."

"Thanks Lee."

"So girls, how was your first week here?" Ethyn asks us. We're sitting in the large common room that everyone uses during our free time between diner and curfew.

"Good." Tess says.

Sadie mumbles, "Meh."

"Alright."

"We survived."

Everyone else has chimed in, but I don't know what to say. "It was interesting."

The other girls nod.

"What do you guys think of those new math formulas we were doing today?" Dave asks to break an awkward silence.

Daniel sighs. "Such a Dave thing to say."

"I hate geometry!" Paige rants. "It doesn't make any sense!"

"It does once you understand the formula," I tell her.

"I'm with Paige," Daniel says.

"Me too," Dawn adds.

"I can help you guys." Dave offers.

"Hey guys! Whatcha talking 'bout?" Zoe asks, sidling up to Dave.

"Umm, nothing that's any of your business," Tess responds, in full on sass mode.

"Who asked you?" Zoe says, returning the sass."

"Well," Sadie starts. "I believe you said 'hey guys whatcha talking 'bout' so technically, any of us could have answered that. Right guys?"

"Right," agrees Tristan, smiling at Sadie.

Is something going on there? Oooohh!

Zoe sits down on the couch basically on top of Dave. He looks really uncomfortable.

"Where are you minions, Zoe?" Tess asks.

Zoe scowls at her. "So Dave, want to hang out sometime? Alone?"

"Um no, actually I don't ever want to hang out with you, especially not alone. Now if you would please get off of me, I'll be going."

Zoe looks stunned, but slowly heads back to her posse.

I catch parts of their conversation.

"-not fair-"

"-know right-"

"-what did they do to get all the hot guys-"

"-look at them-"

"-ugh"

After Dave leaves, the rest of us head back to our rooms.

Tess is weirdly quiet as we get ready for bed.

"You okay, Tess?"

"Yeah, fine. Just tired."

"Okay."

We finish getting ready for bed. Just as I shut off the lights, Tess speaks up. "Amber, did you ever have a boyfriend?"

"Sort of," I mumble.

She is quiet. "Goodnight," I say.

Tess' question made me think of Jackson. Wow. That was a while ago.

At the start of grade nine, Tasha and I were loners. We kept to ourselves, convinced that we didn't need other friends. Then Tasha caught the eye of Nolan, and she fell under his spell. Nolan and Jackson were like Tasha and I. A pair of best friends with no other friends. It was good we met each other. When Tasha and Nolan started dating, Jackson and I talked more. Once the other two were dating, the four of us going to see a movie together was a date for Tasha and Nolan. So Jackson and I sort of started dating. We knew we wouldn't last, but I loved him. When Nolan cheated on Tasha, we ditched the boys. Tasha didn't know Jackson and I were dating, and I never told her. A day later Jackson started dating Kendra, the Barbie doll of the high school. Tasha moved on too. Before Nolan, there was Liam, and after, there was Troy and then Jack.

With this trip down boyfriend lane, I'm hit with how much I miss my crazy best friend. I think of all our great memories together. Like 'The Celebrity Day.'

Tasha and I had gone to the mall, just to hang out. At the mall, a choir started doing a flash mob. Tasha jumped right in and dragged me with her. I stood like a stick, and she did a crazy version of the chicken dance while pretending to know the words. When the choir's conductor showed up and started conducting, we ran for the hills, laughing our heads off.

I never thought I'd be homesick, but I am. I roll over and try to sleep.

The digital clock beside my bedside reads 1:23am. I've been tossing and turning since 10:30! Why can't I sleep? I'm exhausted!

I'll go to the bathroom and get some water.

I stealth out of our room, and down the hall to the bathroom. As soon as I enter the bathroom, I heard quiet crying. I cautiously step in, and look around. Against the back wall there is a petite girl curled up in a ball, crying. I walk over to her.

"Are you okay?"

She looks up at me.

"Am I skinny?" She asks me.

"Yes. And beautiful." I tell her. And it's true. She's stick thin, but gorgeous. She has thick dark hair, clear, pale skin, and deep brown eyes.

"Really? I feel so fat!" She cries.

I sit down next to her. "It's okay," I whisper. "You're not fat at all." I pause. "What's your name? I'm Amber."

"I'm Aria. You're the one that teased Zoe at breakfast that day."

"Yep, that's me." I laugh, and Aria joins in.

"I'm sorry I'm bugging you."

"You're not bugging me at all. I was tossing and turning in bed. I'm not really sure why I came out here."

"I was crying, and my roommate kicked me out."

"Who's your roommate?"

"Erica," she tells me.

"Oh, Duckface?"

Aria bursts out laughing. "She does look like a duck!"

"Yup." I say, chuckling.

"You gonna be okay?" I ask, after we stop laughing.

"Yeah. Being here is just hard for me. I'm anorexic." Aria pauses. "Wow. I can't believe I just said that so bluntly. But yeah. I had help at home, and I don't have anyone here."

I put an arm around her. "You'll be alright."

"Thanks Amber. I really appreciate all this."

"It's no problem."

"But thanks. Goodnight Amber."

We both head back to our dorms. I sneak through the door.

"What are you doing?" Tess croaks from her bed. "It's 1:55am."

"I know. I couldn't sleep, and I went to the bathroom for a while."

"Oh."

I crawl under my covers and lay down my head.

"Goodnight Amber."

"Night."

My favourite sound. The ADCCG bell. Yay!

Once again it interrupts my reading of The House of the Scorpion.

I was at Chapter 12, where Tom forces Matt to discover 'the thing at the hospital.'

Why does class always end when I'm at the good parts?

I stand up and walk to the cafeteria. I am proud to say that I can now navigate my way to and from my classroom and the cafeteria.

Sadie and I get line for food talking about El Patrón and his plans.

I grab a tray and load it with a turkey sandwich, cucumber slices, an apple and chips. Paige joins Sadie and I as we head to the table, the two of them starting an argument about whether Celia has good intentions or not. Paige thinks she's just a pawn in some mastermind plan, Sadie thinks she is the mastermind.

As the two of them discuss these possibilities, I see Aria, carrying a tray with nothing but a small salad on it.

I am struck with the urge to go over and see how she's doing, but I can already tell that Tess will be judgemental of her. I don't want to not sit with the gang of friends we seem to have assembled.

I continue to watch Aria as she sits down beside the '55 boy with the speech impairment.

Hmm. Interesting pair.

Just as this crosses my mind, I walk straight into a table of 19 year olds, drawn in '51 and '52.

I turn bright red. "Oh. Uh-uh. I- Sorry." I look at the 19 year olds, assuming they'll be laughing at me. They're not. One of them is looking at me with a quizzical expression. He almost looks familiar.

"Mitchel?" I ask, at the same time he asks, "Amber?"

"Yeah." I say. Mitchel gets up and hugs me. I awkwardly hug him back.

"How was Tasha?" He asks me.

"She was alright. Really sad."

"Yeah..." He says, trailing off. Then he looks to his friends. "Guys, this is Amber. We're both from Manitoba. My little sister was her best friend."

There's a chorus of Hi Ambers.

Mitchel and I stand awkwardly for a little longer.

"Well," I say. "I better go. See you around."

"Yeah. See you Amber."

I head back over to my table.

"Who was that?" Dave asks.

"He's hot!" Tess chimes in.

Oliver looks up. "Ex boyfriend?"

Tristan slaps him upside the head. "Idiot! They hugged!"

"Were you guys spying?" I joke.

"Yup. Shamelessly." Dawn smiles.

"His name is Mitchel. He was drawn five years ago. He's my bestfriend's brother. Anything else you need to know?"

"Is he single?"

"Really Tess? How would I know? This is the first time I've seen him in five years!"

"Girls. It's okay," Tristan says, sensing tension.

Our table goes quiet. After a moment Dave restarts a conversation, but Tess and I stay quiet. I don't know what just happened between us. She was getting in my nerves, like she sometimes does, but this time, I just snapped.

+++

It's evening free time now, and things between Tess and I are still really awkward.

I head into the large main common room and take a seat on a couch by myself. This is the first time I've actually been alone today, and it feels good.

I'm thinking about whatever happened back there between Tess and I, when someone calls my name.

"Amber! Come 'ere!"

I look around the room. When I see Mitchel, he motions for me to come over to where him and his friends are.

I slowly stand up, and head over to Mitchel and his friends.

"Hey," I say meekly as I walk up to Mitchel's group of friends.

"Hey Amber. I wanted to you to meet my friends."

I nod.

"This is Eve, and Trey, and..."

Names and faces blur together as Mitchel introduces me to his friends.

"And last but not least, my girlfriend, Kendra."

"Hi," Kendra gives a little wave.

I smile shyly at her.

"Amber, I just wanted to let you know that if you need anything thing here, I'm always around. You're kind of like my second little sister," he says with a boyish grin.

I smile again, this time a big genuine one.

"Thanks Mitchel."

"No problem Amber. Go have fun with your friends."

I head back to my couch, and see that Daniel has taken a seat there. Do I want to go sit with him?

I look around the room. Tess is flirting with Oliver, and none of my other friends are here.

Okay, I guess I'll go sit with Daniel.

I'm still confused from truth or dare night. I don't know if he likes me. And what if I have a crush on him?

"Hey Amber," Daniel says, moving over on the couch.

I sit down. "Hi."

"How's it going?" He asks me.

"Pretty good. You?" Wow. This is basically how all my awkward text conversations with Jackson started.

"I'm doing well," Daniel tells me.

I don't know what to say, so I just don't say anything. Great strategy, I know.

Daniel looks at Tess, boldly flirting with Oliver.

"You think she likes him?" He asks.

"Nice observation Sherlock."

Daniel sighs. "Just trying to make conversation, Amber. Jeez."

"Can you make conversation without making the most stupid and obvious statements known to mankind?" I snap.

Daniel looks at me, stunned.

I realize what I've just said. "Daniel, I am so sorry. I don't know what's wrong with me today. I've been snappy at everyone." I apologize.

"Your time of the month?" He jokes.

I blush. "Shut up."

+++

Free time is over now, and Tess and I are getting ready for bed in our room.

"He's got a girlfriend by the way," I tell her.

Tess nods. "Sorry if I was being really annoying like that. I felt bad. I used to be like that all the time at home. Total QB, 24/7. I'm trying to ditch those ways though. I'm sorry."

"I'm sorry too. I shouldn't have snapped at you like that. I did the same to Daniel a little while ago. I don't know what's gotten into me."

"Your time of the month?" Tess jokes.

I groan. "If I hear someone tell me that one more time...ugh!"

"Time of the month!" Tess sings. "Amber's time of the month! La la la la! Time of the month!"

Lee and Marigold clearly her Tess's singing and pop their heads in our room.

"Someone's time of the month?" Marigold asks.

"You guys need anything?" Lee asks us.

"No," I say. "We're good. Tess just needs to shut up."

"Okay," Marigold smiles. The pair leaves, and Tess and I dissolve into a fit of giggles.

Once we settle down, Tess speaks. "In all seriousness, who else said that to you? Is there any but kicking for me to do?"

"Daniel was teasing me after I apologized. It's all good."

"Ohh Daniel! He totally has the hots for you Amber!"

I groan. "Tess!" I complain.

"Love ya!"

"What about Oliver?" I ask.

"I don't know if he's interested." She says.

"Hmm," I nod.

"I'm getting tired, wanna turn off the lights?"

"Yeah. Goodnight Tess."

"Night Amber."

+++

-11-

I'm sitting in the classroom, pondering life and existence.

Ten minutes ago when I entered the classroom the message board read this:

'55 and '56. Please complete the math work page on your desk, and then use the rest of today's class to finish The House of the Scorpion. You must have the book finished by tomorrow. The bell will dismiss you.

I quickly finished the page of easy two step algebra problems, and then read the two chapters I had left in the book.

Now my mind is everywhere. Particularly my family.

Ty, and how he always wanted a piggyback ride. My parents, their unconditional love for the whole family, and willingness to talk. Wait. Talk. That conversation I overheard my parents having the night after I took the test the first time.

"David, what will we do if she's drawn?! I couldn't bear to go through it again!" My mother said, freaking out.

"Shhh Penelope. It's okay." My father calmed her, as always. She was the dramatic one, him the calm, steady one that held us together.

"No! Honey, it's not okay! I worked with her; I told her how she could fail the examination! I cannot do this again!" My mother's voice escalated. But what did she mean by saying 'again'?

"Penelope," my dad murmured softly, as he always did when calming my mother. It almost always worked. "Maybe this is what she wants." Yes Dad. I did want it.

"No! That's not possible! How could she want it?" My mother continued to wail. "She would become government property! How could anyone want that?!" I don't know mom, but I did.

"Dear, if she doesn't want it, I'm sure she'll talk someone into volunteering for her. But if she does go, she'll do well doing whatever the GovChildren do. She's a tough cookie, Amber is. Don't stress it too much," my father reasoned.

"But David, how can you say this? How can be so calm, when we might be losing another child?" What did she mean? I am their firstborn.

"I would be sad to see Amber go, Penelope. Just like I was sad when-"

That's when the air conditioning cut in. If only I had heard what my father said next.

And then there was the story of how my mother got the dress I wore to the draw, the story she never got a chance to tell me.

"Oh Amber! You look gorgeous!" My mother said as she entered my room.

"I love this dress so much!" I exclaimed. "Where did you get it?" I asked, knowing that it couldn't have been cheap.

"It's a special dress that I've had for a long time. Maybe one day I'll tell you the story," Mom said.

If only she had told me the story then. I wish I knew.

I look up around the classroom and see that Tristan, done the work, is also starting into space. I grab one of the extra sheets of paper that was given to show our work and write a note.

Hey -A

I crumple the paper into a ball and lob it, landing it perfectly on his desk. Tasha and I had perfected this back in Winnipeg, and could land notes on each other's desks even with several desks between us.

Tristan looks up, startled, when the paper ball hits his desk.

But he unfolds it and writes back. He crumpled the paper and throws it back, landing it on my desk.

Hey. He wrote.

Finished the work? -A I write.

Tristan writes back, throws, and the paper ball bounces way off my desk.

Smooth, I mouth, smiling. Tristan blushes, and I grab the paper.

Yup. Not very hard. -T He wrote.

I know. When does this class end? -A I write, and send the paper back to Tristan.

I unfold the paper, hoping to find out when class ends.

"When the bell goes." That's a direct quote from Ms Attary herself. -T

No luck.

Thanks Ms Attary. -A

I chuck the ball of paper at him.

Play nice now :) -T

Don't you tell me to play nice. I'll play how I want. -A

Tristan snickers when he opens the paper. His smile grows as he writes a response.

Feisty! Just how I like 'em. -T

I burst out laughing. A few people give me strange looks, and Zach shushes me, but I pay no attention to nerd boy. I'm focused on a good rebuttal.

Slowly, carefully and deliberately, I write my response. I look to Tristan, and he has that Uh-Oh look on his face.

Well, I guess you could go talk to Zoe, heard she's got quite the sass. -A Is what I end up writing.

Tristan painstakingly unfolds the paper, and gets a look of disgust on his face when he reads it.

Seconds later, the paper is back on my desk.

Watch your back Amber. -T

Ha. -A

Tristan stares at the paper for a while before thinking of a response.

How about a truce? -T

I can do that.

Okay -A

So. What now? -T

I don't know -A

Tristan stares at the paper for a while. Then the bell goes. Tristan and I are the first ones standing.

"Problem solved," he says with a grin.

We walk out of the classroom together.

"I have a question." I say.

"Yeah?"

"Is there like a library or something here?"

"Yeah," he says. "Want me to show you?"

"That'd be great. We don't have anymore classes today, do we?" I ask.

"Not until after lunch."

"K."

"Let's go. It's this way," Tristan says, leading me down a new hallway.

We go through a set of doors, and enter the library.

"Wow," I say. This is unlike any library I've ever been to. There's bookshelf of books, a bunch of computers, presumably for our use, and a large book, on a pedestal type thing.

I look around, and then look to Tristan. "Is there a book with all the names that have been drawn?" I ask him.

"Right on the pedestal," he directs me. "Anything you looking for in particular?"

"Do you promise not to tell anyone?" I ask, deciding that Tristan is trustworthy.

"Of course."

"Okay, so the night after I did the ADCCG test the first time, I overheard my parents having a conversation that really confused me. They were talking about how they might lose me. Then my mom said she couldn't bear to go through it again. And I don't know what she means by again, because as far as I know, I'm their firstborn. But I wanted to see if there was someone else with my last name drawn from Manitoba."

Tristan nods. "I'll help."

"Thanks."

We head over to the pedestal, and I open the books to the last page and see my name among the other twelve girls. One page back, and I see the boys names. I keep on flipping back until I see a name that stands out.

Matlock, GreysonManitoba2045

"That must be my brother!" I exclaim.

"Yeah. But you were born in 2041, right? So you were four when he was drawn. That doesn't make sense. You would at least have some memory of him." Tristan points out.

"If he was drawn at age fourteen in 2045, how old is he now?" I ask Tristan.

"25."

"Do you have any idea where we could find him?" I ask.

"I don't know. I guess we'll just have to ask around."

"But we can't be obvious about it. We don't want people getting suspicious."

"Yeah," he agrees.

I stare at the page longer.

Matlock, GreysonManitoba2045

"Ready to go?" Tristan asks me.

"Yeah."

"Let's go."

We head back. I am silent, my head overflowing with information.

"You okay Amber?" Asks Tristan. "You look really pale."

"I think I just need to sit down for a minute," I respond.

Tristan leads me to a couch. I sit down, and he sits down beside me. Tentatively, he puts an arm around me. I don't fight it, and lean in a little bit. Tess is wrong. I don't like Daniel. Now I'm sure of it.

Words swirl around my head. Matlock, Greyson. Greyson Matlock. Manitoba. 2045. Matlock, Greyson. Greyson Matlock. Manitoba. 2045. Matlock, Greyson. Greyson Matlock. Manitoba. 2045. Matlock, Greyson. Greyson Matlock. Manitoba. 2045.

"Amber, Amber. Wake up."

"What?" I open my eyes to see Tristan's smiling face.

"Hey sleeping beauty."

I blush. "Hey."

"It's lunchtime," Tristan tells me.

"How long was I asleep for?" I ask.

"About an hour," he tells me.

He sat like that, with my leaning on him, for an hour? Ohmygosh! That'sso nice! I'm falling for him. Falling hard.

We get up and walk into the cafeteria. I feel like I'm walking on air. He must like me too!

+12+

∧ The song up there is a cover of Ed Sheeran's Photograph, sung by Tyler Ward and Anna Clendening. I love it so much!

"Where were you guys?" Daniel asks Tristan and I when we sit down at the lunch table.

"I showed Amber the library." Tristan says.

"The library?" Sadie asks.

"Seriously?" Asks Oliver, disgusted. He continues. "That place is effing boring!"

"It's not that bad!" Insists Dave.

"Well," Oliver starts, "You are a nerd."

Sadie bursts out laughing.

"What?" asks Oliver. "I'm dead serious! It wasn't supposed to be funny!"

"But it is!" She insists through fits of giggles.

"What were you even doing in there anyway?" Daniel cuts in, harshly.

"I just wanted to know if there was a library. And when I asked Tristan he offered to show me." I tell him. Why does he care.

"You know you could have asked me. Also, why did that take over an hour?"

Jeez. What is his problem? Man period? What the heck.

Tristan speaks up. "Amber looked around. I wanted to check how many points I had, but the computer was being super slow. Then I had to meet my mentor at the pool for a while, and Amber didn't know how to get back here from the library, so she came with me," he says in a rush.

Daniel sighs and mutters under his breath.

"What's your problem, man?" Dave asks.

"Yeah. Seriously Dan, why do you care?" Oliver asks.

"Amber," Daniel says. "Can we talk?"

"Sure," I say. "What's up?"

He leans across the table. "I mean, like, in private?"

"Oh. I guess, yeah."

Daniel stands up, and I follow him out the doors of the cafeteria.

I turn to face him. "What's up?"

"Well, uh,"

"Daniel? Spit it out." I say.

"Where did Tristan actually take you? His bed?"

"Daniel! What the heck! Why do you even care? Honestly, you're being such a possessive jerk right now! We're not dating!"

"Jeez girl. Calm down! I'm helping you!"

"Helping me with what Daniel?" I retort. I've had enough.

He speaks in a quieter tone. "So you didn't actually go to the library?"

"We did! Seriously Daniel? Like, why do you even care?"

"Am I not allowed to care? Come on Amber."

"What do you want!" I shout. "Please! Just-" I stop. "Why do you care?" I say meekly.

"I'm looking out for you Amber."

"But why? Tristan is one of your friends! Don't you trust him? What kind of friendship is that?"

"Amber, I just-"

"Daniel! Just explain!"

He looks down. "I just don't like seeing you with him Amber. I know you could do far better." He pauses. "Amber. I like you."

What? Now? After all Tristan has just done for me? What do I do? What do I say? Where's Tasha? She'd know what to do.

Do I like Daniel?

Or Tristan?

I don't know!

"Uhm. I, uh. I've got to go. Uh, see you later!" I turn on my heel, and head to my room.

I lay down on my bed, overwhelmed. This is just too much right now. First finding out about Greyson, then Tristan, now this with Daniel.

I know who I can go talk to. Maybe he gives advice as good as his sister.

I hop off of my bed and head back to the common room, hoping neither Tristan nor Daniel are present.

I walk through the doors and scan the room. No one my age is here, which is perfect.

Finally, I spot who I'm looking for. I head over.

"Amber! Hey!" Mitchel calls out.

Kendra, his girlfriend, smiles at me and says, "Hey Amber."

"What's up lil 'sis'?"

"Umm, just having problems I guess?"

"Girl stuff?" Mitchel asks.

"Sorta."

"Well, I know I said you can always come find me when you need something, but girl stuff may be more Kenny's specialty." He smiles at his girlfriend.

"Well, it's not the girl stuff that's important. It's something else. Is there somewhere more private we can go?"

"Yeah. Is it okay if Kenny comes along?"

"Yeah."

"Come on, follow me," Mitchel says, taking Kendra's hand.

We go through many hallways, and end up in an old storage room.

"What's up Amber?" Mitchel asks me.

"Greyson Matlock."

"Ahh, you found out?" Mitchel speculates.

"You know about him?"

"Yes. I was eight when he was drawn."

"I was four. How come I don't remember him?" I ask.

"Well," Mitchel starts.

Kendra speaks up. "The circumstances were different back then."

"They made it so you forgot him." Mitchel finishes.

"What?"

Mitchel looks to Kendra. "The ADCCG has changed a lot over the years." She explains simply.

"Do you know Greyson?" I ask them.

"Yes. You could meet him if you want," Mitchel tells me. "He remembers you."

"I'd like to meet him." I say.

"Okay. I can arrange that," Mitchel says.

"Anything else, Amber?" Kendra asks. I like her. She seems to really care, and is super nice.

"No, I think I'm good thanks."

She sends me a concerned glance. "Well, we're always here if you need us."

"Not literally," Mitchel buts in.

Kendra laughs and shakes her head. "No, Mitchel, obviously we aren't always in this exact space, but you know what I mean. Idiot."

"But you love me anyways."

"Ahem," I clear my throat to get their attention. They're really cute together, but I can only take so much lovey dovey stuff, especially when I'm so confused.

"Sorry Amber. Let's get back now," Mitchel says.

+++

I've been laying in bed for over an hour, but I just can't settle down. My brain is going crazy.

I get up out of bed and head to the bathroom.

I push the door open and see Aria sitting in the same spot she was the last time. I walk over and wordlessly sit down beside her.

"Hey."

I smile.

"Hey," I say.

"What's up?"

"Can't sleep," I say simply.

"Same," Aria says.

"How's Duckface?" I ask with a smile.

She laughs. "Just peachy. Tonight she didn't kick me out though. I came out of my own free will."

"And you seem a lot happier," I point out.

"Yeah. It's still hard. I've made a friend though. We're kind of the two misfits."

"Yeah?"

"Yeah," she says. "His name is Quinn. He's the 55 boy with the speech problem."

"Oh, I know who you're talking about."

"What's up with you? You seem to to have a lot on your mind."

"It's pretty complicated."

"I got time," she smiles.

"Okay. Well, awhile ago, Daniel kind of acted like he liked me. But then he dared Tess, my roommate, to kiss him. I was really confused then, cause I didn't know if I like him. Then I got over it and it became normal-just friends. Then today I asked Tristan to show me the library. He took me there, and then I wasn't feeling great, so he took me to a couch in the common room. I fell asleep on his shoulder for about an hour. Then we went to lunch and Daniel was all mad, and asking where we were. Then, we went to talk in private, and he said that I deserve better, and that he likes me."

"So Daniel basically said Tristan isn't good enough for you, but he is? What a jerk."

"Yeah."

"Wow."

"What do I do?" I ask.

"Well, I would say that you need to spend time with both of them, find out if Tristan likes you, and then decide who you like."

I nod.

We sit in silence for a while, and then Aria speaks again. "I think I'm gonna go back to sleep now. I'm really tired."

"Okay. Thanks Aria."

"For what?"

"Being you."

-13-

I sneak out of my bed and into the bathroom. It's been two nights since I had that conversation with Aria. She wasn't there last night.

I open up the door and look around. She's not here tonight either. I guess it's a good thing. It means at least one of us is getting sleep. But it feels lonely. I've enjoyed our late night conversations.

I sit down against the wall where I've sat with Aria. I pull my knees up to my chest and just sit there.

My whole life has changed in a week and a half. Two weeks ago, I was living a normal life. I had friends. Beth, Maddy, Joanne, Ashlyn and of course Tasha. I really do miss them.

"Amber?" a voice asks from the door of the bathroom.

I look up. "Tess? You aren't asleep?"

"No. I was worried about you. Are you okay?"

"Meh."

"What's up? Miss your family?"

"Yeah."

"Other problems?"

"Sorta."

"Like what?"

"Stuff."

"Amber. Really! A week ago, when we first got here we were like, best friends. Now you reply to me in one word sentences and can't even make eye contact with me. What's changed?" She asks, her voice breaking at the end.

Tess looks really sad. I feel bad for her.

"Tess, I- I just. I don't know!"

"Amber. Obviously something is wrong. What is it that's so terrible that you can't bear to tell me about?"

"When we first got here, we were roommates and best friends. We were telling each other everything."

Tess's face contorts when I say 'everything.'

What else was she keeping from me?

But I continue. "Then we started having little disagreements. You wouldn't let me borrow that navy shirt,-"

"So you hate me over a shirt? What the heck Amber! I didn't think you where that shallow!"

"It's not just the shirt thing Tess! Let me talk! Then when I saw Mitchel, we fought about that. All you cared was whether or not he was single, and I was overwhelmed by what was happening. Then I thought we made up that night. You opened up to me about your past, we talked. I thought things were getting better. And now we're here. I just don't know want to do or say Tess."

"We fix it," she says simply.

"But how?" I ask. "Why? Is it even worth it? I don't know what the point is Tess."

Tess sighs. "I guess it's for the better," she says, almost as if she never meant to fix this messed up friendship, and leaves the bathroom.

What have we done?

The clock beside my bedside now reads 3:39am. I haven't slept all night, and it'll catch up to me pretty quickly in this morning's classes. I know I need to sleep, but I can't. There's too much on my mind.

Why was the ADCCG created? That's all I wanted to know before. Now I've all but forgotten that goal. Why does the government need us? It's so confusing. This could be a movie. There's so much drama, it's basically just like we're at a small, rich, weird, boarding school.

I roll over and try, yet again, to get some sleep.

What feels like only five minutes later, the ADCCG alarm clock in our room rings. Turns out I actually got four hours of sleep, as its 7:40am now.

Tess and I silently get dressed and head out in to the common room. Tess is talking to Oliver and Daniel, so I go stand beside Tristan.

"Hey Amber," he says, his face brightening.

"Hey," I say with a smile.

"What's up?"

"Tess and I are fighting."

"Aw, that sucks. Anything can do to make it better?"

"Talking to you is making me feel better," I say shyly. This is as close as I come to flirting.

He smiles. "Good."

"I wonder what's for breakfast. I'm hungry."

"I don't know," Tristan says.

Just as he finishes speaking, the cafeteria doors open and the common room starts emptying.

"I guess we're going to find out," I say.

When we get into the cafeteria I can smell good breakfast food.

I grab a tray, and load it with apple juice, a bagel, watermelon and bacon. Tristan and I head to our group's usual table. It'll be a little awkward between me and Tess, but I have no where else to sit.

"You gonna be okay sitting over here?" Tristan asks me.

"Yeah. Thanks though."

We sit down and I end up between Tristan and Daniel. Great. Let's just confuse Amber some more.

While we eat, all of us are pretty quiet. But all of a sudden the whole cafeteria goes quiet. I look around, and see Ms Attary strutting into the cafeteria.

"Good morning. I'm sure you're all curious as to what I'm doing here. I have an announcement that I think will please you. We will be having a dance next week. For those of you that are new here, you can find out more information from your mentors and friends. Have a nice day." And with that, she leaves.

After the cafeteria door closes the room erupts into chatter.

"A dance?" Paige asks.

All of us girls are equally confused.

"Why do the give us dances?" I ask.

"If this place was torturous, they have people trying to break out left and right. By giving us fun things and education, it keeps us happy," Dave explains.

Oliver pipes up. "There you have it folks. The smart, Dave answer."

"It's not really complicated," Ethyn says.

"Nah, Oliver's just too stupid," Tristan says, laughing.

"Hey! Watch it!" Oliver says to Tristan, pretending to be mad, and failing.

Everyone starts laughing at Oliver's failed acting attempt.

"Weren't an actor back at home, were you?" Dawn asks.

"Maybe I was! Maybe I was destined for a Grammy award!" Oliver insists.

"You do realize that the Grammy's are for music, right?" I ask, through laughter. And with that, the whole table is in fits of laughter again.

Tristan holds out his hand for a high five. I smile and slap his hand.

"But really," Dave says. "To answer the dance question, their goal is to keep this place like a small, fancy, boarding school. Don't ask how I know that, because I can't tell you."

"Do you know why we're here?" I ask.

"No idea," Dave tells me. "That's one thing I haven't figured out."

I nod. Everyone starts guessing why we're here. I sit quietly, lost in thought.

Finally an update! So sorry about the long wait. School started, and BOOM, I no longer had spare time.

It was 's comment that actually forced me to write this chapter for you guys, I had finally gotten an idea into my head, but didn't feel like writing it, and then I read her comment and forced myself to start writing.

Anyway, I'm really excited to write the next few chapters. If school doesn't murder me they should be up soonish.

So yeah. Vote and comment, love you guys!

Jen

PS-song at the top is Taylor Swift's Wildest Dreams. Learning that on piano was another reason for the slow update. *sheepishly grins*

+14+

Hey guys! Just want to clear things up. Depending on when you read chapter 13, it may have said that the dance was in a month or a week. The dance is in a week, and should be chapter 15!!

Also, the picture up there has to relevance, it's just a cool picture I took at my cabin.

"A dance, huh?"

Tristan smiles. "Yup. We get them once and a while."

"Are they fun?"

"They're not bad. You go to dances back at home?"

"Only once. I never had anyone to go with."

"Seriously? You didn't have a date? Wow."

I blush. "What about you?" I ask. "Did you go to dances? Have girlfriends?"

"Not really. I was in grade nine during the draw. I went to one high school dance, but then we broke up when my name went in the bowl."

"Awh. That sucks."

"She understood. I couldn't do what Dave did."

"Yeah, I know."

We both get quiet, listening to the conversation around the table. We've long finished eating our breakfast, but we don't have classes today, so we're still hanging out here at our lunch table, talking.

I look around the table.

Paige and Dawn are talking with Dave, Tess and Oliver are flirting, Sadie and Ethyn are talking with Daniel half in the conversation, and Tristan and I are just sitting, quietly.

Sadie and Ethyn stand up. "Let's go to the common room," Sadie says. "The couches are comfier."

"Okay," Tess agrees.

Everyone stands up, and we head over there. I linger behind a little bit, enjoying the calm and quiet.

I look over to the large wall with white blinds pulled down over all the large windows. Curious, I head over, and cautiously pull one of the blinds forward a little. No alarm goes off, so I pull the blind forward more, and peek around it.

I'm slightly disappointed to see that it's just a courtyard, nothing that could tell me where we are, but it's still outdoors.

I hear someone enter, and I drop the blind, letting it fall back into place, and take a step back.

"Amber?" asks a familiar voice.

Daniel.

"Hi," I say.

"Looking outside?"

"Yeah, I guess."

"Want to go outside?" he offers.

"Sure." I say. It's a sweet gesture, and even though he's given so many mixed signals, I'm willing to take it.

"Follow me."

We head down another unfamiliar hallway, and then go up a flight of stairs. We walk further, then down another flight of stairs and to a door marked emergency exit.

"Can we go through there?" I ask hesitantly.

"Yeah, it's safe, promise."

"Okay."

Daniel pushes open the door, and nothing bad happens. He holds it open for me and gestures for me to go ahead. I step through, and trip, not realizing that there's a step down.

"Oh Amber! I'm sorry! I forgot to warn you that there's a step. I'm so sorry. Are you okay?" Daniel holds out a hand, and I graciously take it.

As he pulls me up, he wraps his other arm around my waist, steadying me.

I smile gratefully, and we walk into the courtyard. Daniel keeps his hand on my waist, which I don't mind, because still feel uncoordinated from falling.

The courtyard is a good size, and we wander around a little while before sitting down on one of the benches.

"Amber, I'm really sor-"

"It's okay Daniel," I cut in. "I'm not hurt, and it's not your fault that I tripped."

"No, not about that. I'm sorry I was being a jerk a few days ago, when Tristan took to you the library. Tristan and I are good friends; I got jealous. I'll try not be rude and jealous, but I can't stop what I feel for you Amber. You're amazing. You've captured my heart and blown my mind in a short amount of time. Maybe I'm disgusting you with cheesiness, but I swear, I'm serious. I can't stop these feeling Amber."

He looks straight at me. "You're beautiful."

I'm speechless. I don't know what to say. He almost sounded sincere, but saying I'm beautiful makes it sound like he only has these feeling because he like the way I look.

"Daniel," I start. "I-ah-I don't know what to say."

"It's okay Amber. You don't have to do anything."

So quickly that I don't even realize what's happening, he leans in and gives me a quick kiss on the lips.

"Ah," I stammer. I'm at a loss for words.

We sit in silence for a while. My mind is racing.

Daniel just kissed me! What do I do? There's a dance next week, there are two guys, what do I do?

I want to scream.

+++

Later, Daniel takes my hand and leads me to the door. It's nearly lunch time. At least Tristan won't throw a fit about me being with Daniel.

I drop Daniel's hand, and then see Tristan coming down the hall.

"Hey Amber," he says with an easy smile.

"Hey," I say, returning the smile.

Daniel tenses up beside me.

I elbow him in the side.

"Hi," he says stiffly.

"What're you guys up to?" Tristan asks, politely, but genuine.

"I don't know. We were in the courtyard, and I'm not sure where we're going now."

Tristan nods. "I was just heading out to get some air, but everyone else is in the common room."

"Okay, thanks." I look to Daniel. "Let's head over there."

Daniel and I enter the bustling common room and head over to our friends. Before we get over to their couches, I hear someone call me.

"Amber! Come 'ere!"

I follow the voice to Mitchel and Kendra.

"Want to meet Greyson?" Mitchel asks me.

"It would have to be short," Kendra says, "but it's possible."

"I'd love to." Just as the words leave my mouth, Daniel reappears at my side.

"There you are! You just disappeared, I couldn't find you!" he exclaims.

"Who's this?" Kendra asks me, a teasing smile on her face.

"Daniel, one of my friends."

Mitchel does the creepy suggestive eyebrow raise thing, and I laugh. "No, not like that."

"Not yet," Daniel says. I blush, but am angry that he would say that.

"K, let's go," I say to Mitchel and Kendra. "See ya later Daniel."

Daniel looks a little confused that I just left him, but I have a brother to meet.

Kendra and Mitchel lead me down a hallway. We take a right and enter a large, but empty, storage room.

"Mitchel?" A guy's voice asks. We step into the room. "Amber?"

A figure steps out of the shadows. He is tall and muscular, with blonde hair, and the same deep brown eyes that Ty and I share.

"Greyson?" I ask hesitantly.

He opens his arms and envelopes me in a hug.

"Amber, I can't believe you're here. It's just. Oh my gosh. How were mom and dad?"

"Mom was really really sad, Dad was more accepting. And Ty, he didn't really know what was going on."

"Ty?"

"Oh yeah, you left when I was four. Sorry. Ty is my-our little brother. He's in kindergarten now."

Greyson look sad. "I missed you, baby sister, and even though I never would wish for you to leave our family, I'm glad you're with me."

I smile. "I'm glad I'm with you."

After beginning to catch up with Greyson, Kendra and Mitchel and I walk back to the common room. It was hard to find a time to see Greyson because apparently once you turn 21, everything's organized way differently.

When we walk into the common room, Tristan sees me and comes over.

"Wow Amber," Kendra smiles. "Lots of admirers you have!"

"Hey Tristan. What's up?"

"Not much. Wanna hang out for a while?"

"Of course," I answer with a smile.

"How do you feel about the library?"

I nod. Tristan smiles and with a grin, says, "Let's hope Daniel doesn't kill us this time."

"He better not, otherwise I'll never hang out with him again."

Tristan laughs and holds the door for me as we leave the common room.

"Thanks," I smile.

"Anytime."

Guys, I am so so sorry that I went like three weeks without an update. I'm also sorry that this is kind of short, but for me, that was the perfect place to end it.

Anyway, I promise I will update sooner next time.

Please comment and vote and make me super happy!

The dance is coming up, who's excited???

Love you amazing readers!!

Jen

PS Happy Thanksgiving my fellow Canadians!! (I know it's not til Monday, but whatever)

-15-

I lean over to Paige in class. "Where's Dawn?"

"Don't know," she says, not sounding too happy about it. "I haven't seen her around lately."

"Hmm. I wonder why."

Paige shrugs, and we go back to our work.

Finally the bell rings, and we are released from the wrath of class.

We head to the cafeteria and heap our plates full of mac and cheese, then head to our table. Dawn is already sitting there with a plate when we get there.

She looks up when we arrive. "Hey guys."

"Where've you been the past few days?" Paige questions.

"Nowhere special," Dawn replies, and goes back to eating.

No one has anything else to say, so we start eating our lunch.

"Do we have classes again after lunch?" Dawn asks, breaking the silence.

"Uh, I don't know," Ethyn says. "Dave?"

"The screen said to head to the library after lunch," Dave tells us.

"Okay," Dawn says, and goes back to eating.

Our table falls into silence once again. I'm thinking of Dawn. Clearly, something's up. Her behaviour right now kind of reminds me of Aria when I first met her. Come to think of it, I haven't seen Aria around lately.

"Dawn," I say. She looks up. "Is everything okay?"

She looks surprised that I've asked. "It will be," she says with a sad smile.

"I'm here if you need me."

"Guys come on. We've gotta get to the library," Dave insists, trying to hurry us up.

"Okay, okay," Tess sighs.

We all push our chairs out, stand up and follow Dave to the library.

There's a sign on the door that says: '55, '56 fitness sign up here

What is that?

I feel a hand hold my arm back, and turn around to see Tristan.

"We did this last year," he tells me.

"What is it?" I question.

"There's a bunch of fitness options, and we choose one to sign up for. It's their way of keeping us fit. We'll be in the one we choose now for about a month, and then choose another one."

I nod in understanding.

"I was just wondering, do you want to sign up for the same one," he pauses, looking almost scared. "Like-cause we're friends-you know?" He blushes.

"Yeah, of course," I say, smiling.

We head into the library, and see everyone crowded around an table that has the sign up sheet on it.

"Let's just wait until they're done," Tristan says to me.

"Good idea."

Once everyone is done, Tristan and head up to the round table.

There is a laptop on the table with our options. I look down the list.

Running-full

Paintball-three spots

Weights-full

Yoga-one spot

Swimming-two spots

Zumba/dance-one spot

Tennis-full

Tristan and I look at each other.

"So."

"Maybe it wasn't the best plan to wait till the end," Tristan says.

I laugh. "It's all good."

"Paintball, swimming, or we could spilt up for dance and yoga," he made a face.

"I'm not doing paintball," I say.

"It's fun!" He insists.

"Fun?" I ask. "More like painful!" I am adamant about not doing paintball. It's something I've always been scared of.

"So, swimming, or we could do disgusting dance and yoga."

"I bet those two are for all the girly girls and un-athletic people."

He laughs. "Definitely. So, swimming?"

"I guess so," I say with fake confidence.

Tristan takes the mouse, clicks on swimming and types our names, taking the last spots.

Thank you, Tristan '55 and Amber '56. Please head to the common room until the announcement to go to your stations.

"Let's go," I say.

Tristan and I head back to the common room. As we enter, I see Aria sneaking out of the common room, to the hallway where the girls dorms are.

"I'll be right back," I tell Tristan. "I have to run to my dorm."

"Okay. I'll be here."

I go through the same doors Aria just went through, and speed walk down the hallway.

I can see Aria in front of me in the hallway. She slows, and takes a seat on one of the couches in the little sitting area that's just for us girls.

"Hey," I say, sitting down beside her.

She jumps. "Oh! Hey Amber!"

"We haven't talked lately," I say. "How's it going?"

"It's alright. I mean, you can't really say we're in a great situation, we were taken away from our families. It's tough, but at least I'm adjusting. Like I said before, Quinn and I hang out."

"Yeah," I say. I feel bad that I have a whole bunch of friends and they just have each other, but most of my friends, save for Tristan and maybe a few others, would not appreciate the presence of Aria and Quinn.

"And how's Duckface?" I ask.

Aria laughs. "Same old, same old."

I join her laughter. It feels good to laugh.

"So," she starts. "How are things goin' with the boys?"

"Well. Yesterday Daniel took me to the courtyard. He was like holding my hand and stuff. It wasn't weird. And then he kissed me. On the lips-"

"Seriously?!"

"Yeah! Then we went inside, to the common room, and I hung out with a guy from Manitoba that I knew; he's a few years older than us. Then Tristan and I went to the library and hung out there for a little bit. Then today when we went to the library to sign up for the athletic things, whatever they're called, Tristan asked if I wanted to do one with him. So we're doing swimming."

"Okay. So do you think Tristan likes you?"

"Honestly, I don't know," I tell her. "I don't even know if Daniel likes me, or if it's all just a charade. When we played truth or dare he dared Tess to kiss him."

"He probably wanted to see your reaction."

"Oh!" I exclaim. "I never even thought of that!"

"I think they both like you. I mean, Daniel is obvious. And I think Tristan is just too scared to admit it."

"I don't know," I say, unsurely. "I think Tristan just wants to be friends."

"No. I think he likes you. And that's my final opinion. Court case closed," Aria claps her hands to mimic banging the gavel.

I start giggling and Aria joins in. Once we start we can't stop.

"I'm really glad we met," Aria says, once we have calmed down.

"Yeah. Me too."

We make conversation for a little while longer, and then the bell goes.

Rrrrrrrrrrrrrrrrrrrrrrr

After the bell, there is an automated voice.

'55 and '56 please report to your fitness stations. Thank you.

"Alright. I guess that's our cue," I say. "Where are you headed?"

"Tennis," Aria tells me. "I didn't want to be in dance or yoga. That's probably where Zoe and all her minions are."

"Good thinking."

We head out to the common room. I really hope Tristan is waiting for me, cause I don't remember how to get to the pool.

Lucky for me, he is waiting there. Aria and I part ways and I walk over to Tristan.

"Thanks for waiting," I say gratefully. "I don't know the way to the pool."

"It's okay. This is a confusing place for the first while."

I nod.

Tristan navigates the halls easily, and we get to the pool in no time. We separate at the change rooms.

I enter the girls change room. Again, there is a variety of bathing suits laid out on the bench. I chose a simple blue tankini top, and black bottoms.

There is no one else in the change room with me. Either I'm the only girl, the other girl or girls are late, or early.

Once I'm changed, reality hits me. I signed up for swimming! What was I thinking?

Lee isn't here to calm me this time.

What is I drown? What if I make a fool of myself? What is Cody is here?

I need to calm down. Tristan is here too. He wanted to do an activity together. He's a good friend.

Calmed, slightly, I walk out to the pool. Standing on the pool deck are four guys, one of them Tristan, and another the lifeguard from last time. There's a random guy, and Cody.

I start freaking out again.

Calm down! You're okay Amber.

I walk over to the group.

"Hey," Tristan says, smiling.

The lifeguard claps his hands. "Okay!" he shouts. "Is everyone here now? Tristan?"

"Here."

"Sam?"

"Here."

"Cody?"

"Yo."

"And Amber."

"Here."

"Alright. I'm Evan, age 21, drawn in '49. I'm the-" he makes air quotes, "Lifeguard here. If you want to get in the pool, I'll have each of you swim two laps, one by one."

We head to the water and hop in.

"You okay Amber?" Tristan asks me.

"Not really."

Tristan looks concerned, so I explain. "I've always had a bit of a fear of water. When we did the mentor activities, Lee and I were kayaking in here-"

Evan claps his hands. "Cody, swim first, then Sam, then Amber and last, Tristan. Just there and back."

I continue. "Cody flipped us. My fear grew. I thought I'd be okay, but now that Cody's here, I'm not too sure."

"It's okay Amber. I'm here, and I won't let Cody do anything to you. I promise."

"Okay. Thank you Tristan."

Sam finishes his laps, and now it's my turn.

"You got this Amber," Tristan encourages.

And I do. I swim the laps, albeit a little slower than the others, but still, I did it.

At the end of the hour, Evan sends us to the change rooms.

I come out of the girls change room feeling really proud of myself.

Tristan is waiting for me when I come out.

"You're slow," he jokes.

"Maybe boys are just too fast."

"Whatever. I'm proud of you, you did really good."

"Thanks. I honestly don't think I could have done it without you there."

"Glad I could be there for you."

Yay!!!!!!

Anyway, another chapter a six days later. , you must be so proud!

Please vote and comment; tell me what you think, it means the world to me Comment a character you'd like to see more of in the upcoming chapters.

Love you guys, thanks for all of your support!

Jen

+16+

"Amber. Tess. Wake up!" a voice whispers.

"Huh?" I ask groggily.

"Up! Now!" I open my eyes and see Lee and Marigold in Tess and my's room.

"What?" Tess asks, sounding concerned.

"Just get dressed and come out," Marigold urges. "Quick!"

I realize that whatever it is, it's important. So I hop out of bed and get dressed, quickly, as always.

Tess is still laying in bed, so I motion for Marigold and Lee to come over to me.

"I have an idea," I whisper. I whisper my idea to them and it puts smiles on their faces. Each of them grab their necessary items, and I grab mine.

We creep over to Tess's bed.

Marigold and Lee smack her across the face with socks, and I hit her with my pillow.

"Up! Up!" We chant.

"Okay! Okay! Enough!" Tess exclaims. "Stop! I'm getting up!"

Tess dresses quickly, and the four of us head out into the girls common area. Everyone is grouped around a portable message board, similar to the ones that are in our classrooms.

The dorms for the '56 girls are being reconfigured.

The new dorm assignments are as follows:

a: Sadie/Zoe

b: Marie/Aria

c: Paige/Erica

d: Ana/Jenna

e: Beatrice/ Maggie

f: Amber/Tess

Thank you for your cooperation in these switches. Please report to the common room after the necessary girls have moved their things. There, there will be instructions on the message board regarding the day.

Everyone seems to be puzzled by the news. I look around, but don't see Sadie out yet.

"Someone's name isn't on the list," states one of the girls from up north, either Jenna or Ana, I don't remember.

"Dawn," I say blankly. Why is she gone?

Sadie enters the room with a tear stained face. "Is it gone?" she asks, sadness evident in her voice. I guess she's referring to the message on the board.

One of the '50 girls shakes her head, and envelopes Sadie in her embrace.

Tess has left my side, and is now talking with Paige. I head over to Aria.

"So," I say. "No more Duckface."

She nods, but both of us know it's not really funny.

"But why did they switch me?" Aria asks. "I mean, they could have just moved Zoe, Paige or Marie into Sadie's dorm, but instead they did a whole bunch of switches."

"I have no idea," I say. "Kind of how I feel about a lot of things around here," I add sadly.

Aria nods in agreement. "Do you know anything about Marie?"

"I have no idea. Ask Paige, they were in the dorm together."

"I never talk to those people, remember?"

"Oh. Yeah."

Aria tried to reassure me by saying, "It's okay, Amber. Don't feel bad. I'm used to it."

But hearing that only makes me feel worse. There's nothing weird about Aria. Sure, she has an eating disorder, but she's a great girl. How can we overlook people in such a way? Were there people in Winnipeg like Aria that I didn't even know existed? All because I was happy having Tasha as a friend, and was convinced I needed no other friends?

"Amber?" Aria asks, sounding really concerned. "Are you okay? You've gone white as a sheet."

"Yeah-uh. Yeah. I'm okay."

"You sure?" She asks, definitely not convinced.

"Certain."

"If you say so."

"Yeah. Let's go to breakfast."

"First I have to move my stuff out of dorm c and into b," she tells me.

"Oh, right." Facepalm. "I'll help you. Then we can go to the common room and see the messages for the rest of the day."

"Sounds like a plan."

We leave the girls area and head into Aria and Duckface's room. Paige is already there with some stuff.

"Oh hey Amber," she says. Then she turns to Aria and says, quite rudely, "Hey, you, move your stuff."

I'm shocked that Paige would be so rude. That's not going to help Aria's problem.

"Amber, how come you're here? I don't need any help getting settled," Paige says, continuing on like she wasn't just incredibly rude to someone.

"I'm helping Aria," I state blankly. Aria grabs one of two piles of stuff and leaves. I take the other pile and hurry out of the room to catch her.

When we enter dorm b, Paige's old bed is empty, Zoe is still packing up her stuff, with the help of her minions. And Marie is just sitting on her bed.

Aria dumps her pile on the empty bed and flees the room. Once again, I rush to catch her, but I don't see her outside in the common room.

Crap. I have to find her. Everyone else is heading out into the main common area, but I have to find Aria.

I go to the bathroom door and open it, hoping this will be easy. But the bathroom is empty.

She wouldn't have fled to the main common room, right?

I check her new room and her old room. Then I head into my room. It's a long shot, but maybe.

I slowly push open the door to my dorm. I hear quiet crying.

"Aria?" I ask. She's sitting cross legged in the middle of the floor. She looks up.

"Aria. I'm so sorry," I say as I take a seat beside her on the floor.

+++

Aria and I walk into the main common room together.

There are still a lot of people in the main area.

There are instructions on the message board, just as the girls board said that there would be.

Hello ADCCG children. Due to unforeseen circumstances, the earlier announced 'dance' is cancelled. The bell will ring when it's time for lunch.

Tristan notices me and comes over to where Aria and I are standing.

"Where were you?" He asks. "I was worried."

"I needed to be with Aria," I tell him. "Aria, this is Tristan. Tristan, Aria."

"Hey," Tristan says kindly.

Aria gives a shy wave. We stand there awkwardly for a minute or so, and then a guy sneaks up behind Aria and puts his hands over her eyes.

She giggles and protests, "Quinn!"

He removes his hands and joins our little 'standing around awkwardly' group.

"Amber, this is my friend Quinn that I told you about." To Quinn, she says, "Quinn, this is Amber, and her friend Tristan."

The boys do their head nod greeting thing. Aria leans over and whispers in my ear. "Quinn has trouble speaking, so he probably won't talk to you right now, it embarrasses him. He often uses sign language or writes things down."

"Okay. Good to know."

We make small talk for a little while and then Tristan asks if we can talk in private.

"Did something weird happen with the girls?" He asks. "No one will say anything."

"Promise not to tell?"

"I swear on my life."

"K. Our mentors woke me and Tess up because everyone else was already awake. We went into the girls common area, and everyone from the '50 girls to our age was there. The dorm assignments were changed because Dawn is gone. Sadie was in tears. And they didn't just put one person from the triple dorm into Sadie's dorm like they did with you guys. They did a whole bunch of rearranging. And now the dance is canceled too." Tristan nods. Then I realize something. "Wait a second. Did we have breakfast?" I ask.

Tristan thinks for a moment. "Nooo...the message says the bell will go at lunch. What the heck?"

"What's going on?" I ask. "This is all so confusing."

Tristan nods again.

"Oh!" I exclaim. "Paige was also really rude to Aria."

"Hmm," is Tristan's response. "Not that I don't like Aria or anything, but when did you guys become friends?"

"Well," I start. "We met a while back in the bathroom, late at night." I see his puzzled expression. "Don't ask. Then we became friends, but for some reason we never talked around everyone else. But today we just did."

"Cool. The others are being kind of weird lately," he observes.

"You've been noticing that too?! I'm not going crazy!"

"No, definitely not. Daniel was all weird with you and now is ignoring you. Tess is fighting with you, and the tries to be your bff. And no one else is normal."

"Yeah. And-"

Someone taps my shoulder. "Amber?" Aria asks. "There's someone looking for you," she motions to Mitchel. Quinn is with her too.

"Hey Mitch," I say. "What's up?"

"You need to come with me and Kendra. We need to talk with 'our friend.'" He must mean Greyson. "It's important." He pauses. "Do you trust them?" He asks, motioning to Tristan, Aria and Quinn.

I know I trust Aria and Tristan. And if Aria and Quinn are friends, then I trust him too.

"Yes," I say. "Definitely."

"Okay. Then they can come too. Come on."

He leads the four of us down a hallway similar to the one we went down when Mitchel and Kendra took me to meet Greyson.

Mitchel opens a door and leads us into a storage room. Kendra, and Greyson and another guy wait inside.

"Hey Amber!" Greyson gets up and gives me a big hug. "How's is going?"

"Meh," I say.

"And who are your friends?" He asks.

I hesitate. "It's okay Amber," Greyson tells me. "I told Mitchel you could bring friends. But just these three. No more."

I nod. "This is Tristan, Quinn and Aria." I say.

Greyson smiles. "I'm Amber's big brother."

"Greyson, right?" Tristan asks.

"Yeah. How did you know?"

"I was with Amber when she found out about you," he explains.

"Oohh."

"So anyway," Greyson says. "To our youngsters, we're here because something weird is happening around here. We often have meetings like this in secret. So I tend to be in charge, this guy here," Greyson says, gesturing to the guy beside him, "Is Jay, that's Mitchel, and that's Kendra. So what exactly happened with the girls this morning?"

Kendra recaps the events of this morning. It is confirmed that there has not been breakfast.

"Well," Jay says, "Like everything else around here, there's not much we can do. Unless-" he pauses and whispers with Greyson, Mitchel and Kendra. It appears that they decide not to tell us whatever it is that is so classified.

+++

We head back into the common room, which is full, because everyone's hanging around there.

Someone looks up when we come back in. "Everything's locked. We can't get back into the dorms. We can't get to the cafeteria. We're stuck here. The message board is empty."

+++

Hey guys! So, I'm really sorry it's been so long without an update. Oops. I've been really busy. Ya know, school.

But I finally wrote a chapter. And it's a long one. So yay!

One of my best friends, , just published a scifi story of her own, Saving the Soulless. Go check it out, it's great!

Have you guys heard the Adele song? Hello? It's so amazing.

CONTEST!!!!!: Who can correctly tell me how old the '50 girls are? Comment, and the first person to get it will be mentioned in the next chapter.

Jen <3

-17-

All the couches and chairs have already been claimed, because everybody is locked in here.

Tristan speaks what I'm thinking. "Guys, we're never going to be able to get a chair or a couch. How about we head over to that corner there. It's quiet and no one will bug us."

Quinn nods, and in unison, Aria and I say okay.

We sit down in the corner, me leaning up against one of the walls with my legs pulled up to my chest, Tristan beside me, sitting with his legs stretched out. Aria and Quinn are up against the other wall, Aria leaning on Quinn.

We talk for a little while, about trivial matters, trying to take our minds off of the situation at hand. I'm not really sure about the others, but it's really not helping me.

Aria starts to doze off, all cuddled up against Quinn. They look so cute.

Why are all the doors locked? And why could we get back into the common room if all the doors are locked? This is all so confusing.

So, so confusing...

I'm in a small room with four bright white walls. One part of the wall has a window, but the other side must be mirrored, because no one on the other side can see me. There's no way out. I pound on the walls, but no one can hear me. I scream until my voice goes hoarse.

"Help me!" I scream at the top of my lungs. "Help me! I'm trapped!"

Through the window, I see Tristan, Greyson and Ty. Also with them is Paige. Paige is standing in front of them, a gun in hand. She is saying something to them, making threats, maybe.

She holds a gun to Ty's head.

"No!" I scream, but they can't hear me. Not my little brother! Please!

I can hear a voice calling my name now.

"Amber," the voice says, "Amber. Amber."

"Stop!" I scream. "Help!"

Paige pulls the trigger, and Ty crumples to the ground.

"Noo! Do something!"

"Amber."

The white room starts to shake. I can still hear my name being called. My shoulders are shaking. "Amber!" the voice calls, with such intensity now.

Then everything looks normal again.

There's the common room, and Aria and Quinn, asleep, leaning on each other.

"Amber?" I look over to see Tristan's face, creased with worry. "Are you okay?" he asks me. "You were screaming in your sleep. I'm surprised you didn't wake anyone up."

"Ah-I-I think I'm okay now. A little shaken up, it was a pretty bad nightmare."

He nods. "Want to talk about it?"

"I was trapped in a white room, and-and- through a window I could see you and Paige and Greyson and my little brother. And-and-and Paige-sh-she had a gun-"

"Shhh Amber. It's okay, I promise. It was just a dream." Tristan wraps an arm around my shoulders protectively and I lean into him.

"She shot my broth-" my voice breaks, and I can't finish the last word. I sob into Tristan's shoulder, and he holds me, letting me cry.

A few minutes later, I've calmed down. My face is stained with tears, but I don't feel quite as terrible now.

I wipe the tears off my face.

"Ya know, if this was some sappy romance movie, I'd be wiping the tears off your face for you."

I giggle.

Tristan gives me a hug. "Feeling a little better now?" He asks. "I know how bad it can be. I had nightmares when I first got here too. It's something about this place."

"Yeah." I pause. Tristan still has his arm draped over my shoulder. "Has anything like this ever happened before? You know, being locked in here?"

"Not that I know of," he says uncertainly.

"Has it always been weird like this around here?"

He shakes his head slowly. "Things are changing."

"So we came here, and screwed everything up?"

"Just changed things, Amber"

"For the worse?"

"I have you now, so it can't possibly be all bad."

I smile. That was so cheesy, but still made my heart melt. I lean into him a little bit, instead of awkwardly sitting like a stick. We sit in silence for a moment, but I have to break it.

"What's gonna happen Tristan? They didn't feed us breakfast, it doesn't look like we're getting lunch. People are going to get grumpy."

He looks sad, but gives me the answer I was expecting. "I really don't know Amber. But your brother is here, and Mitchel, and Kendra and lots of other people. We're going to be okay."

It isn't much, but it reassures me a little.

"Do you miss your family?" I ask.

"Of course I do."

I must have a thoughtful look on my face or something, because he looks at me and asks, "Whats wrong?"

"It's just that, like, my brother is here. I have family here, and another person I grew up with is here. But I still miss my family and friends. A lot. And it makes me feel bad, because I already have more than most people here."

"You can't feel bad about missing your family Amber. Everyone does. People go to a sleepover at a friend's house, where they know and trust everyone there, and they still miss their parents. Yes, you are lucky that people from you life are here, but that doesn't mean you aren't allowed to miss your family."

I nod. "Thanks. One more question. Where did you come from?"

"BC."

Judging by the short answer, I'm guessing he doesn't want to talk about it.

Both Tristan and Quinn are sleeping now.

"You guys are so adorable!" Aria whispers, sounding super excited.

I stick my tongue out at her. "Says you. You and Quinn are way cuter."

She giggles. "We are, aren't we?"

I join her quiet laughter. "So Daniel's finally out of the picture?" she asks.

Just as she says it, I see him walking toward us. "Speak of the devil," I whisper.

"Literally," she hisses under her breath.

"Hello ladies," Daniel says. To Aria, he says, "May I steal Amber away from you for a moment."

"Hmmmm," she says. Anyone else, including Daniel, would think she's just teasing, but I can tell that she's honestly thinking about saying no. "I guess if you must, then you can take her. I don't like you though."

He laughs, thinking that this too is a joke. I get up and follow him a little ways a way, where we can talk in private.

"What?" I ask, wanting to get this over with. I feel nothing with him. Tristan on the other hand...that's another story.

"Jeez. So rude. Nothing like the Amber who kissed me in the courtyard."

Ohmygosh! I didn't kiss him! He kissed me! Is he going to spin it around like this? Piece of crap.

"Excuse me?" I ask. Full on sass queen mode.

"Ya know, when you grabbed my face and forced a nasty kiss on me?"

"Excuse me? You little-"

"Oh Amber, don't be like this. Feisty doesn't suit you. You can't have me, sweetie. But, you can go back to itty bitty baby Tristan, knowing that I was your first," he pauses and kisses me roughly, "and second, kiss."

I am going to kill him.

I try to kick him where the sun don't shine, but he anticipates it and pushes my foot away as if he's swatting away a fly. I spin around on my heel and head back to our corner fuming.

As I return, Aria looks puzzled, but that's not what makes the situation worse. Tristan is awake, and looks incredibly disappointed.

Aria gets up and walks toward me, a mix of concern and confusion on her face.

"Amber? What the heck happened over there?" She's not using a mad tone; good to know someone isn't mad at me. She just sounds so confused.

"Come, let me explain," I say, and we head back to where Daniel and I were, just mere moments ago.

"So?" She asks expectantly.

"I'm going to kill him!" I rage.

"K. Amber," she places a hand on my should. "Calm down. We can murder him later."

I smile at that.

"But really," she says. "Tell me what happened."

"When we got over here I was like, 'what do you want,' and he said how rude I was, and that that's nothing like the Amber the kisses him in the courtyard. But I didn't freakin kiss him! He kissed me! So I said 'excuse me?' and he went on and on about how I kissed him and how nasty it was. Then he said that I could go back to Tristan, and I'm thinking 'finally. I can get away from you now' and then he adds that I can go back to Tristan knowing that he was my first kiss. And then, as I'm assuming you guys saw, he kissed me, and then pointed out that he's my second kiss too."

"That little-"

"Aria. Please. Did Tristan see?"

She nods slowly. "From our angle, Daniel made it look like you were kissing him too. Tristan's pretty hurt. He really likes you Amber."

I'm devastated. I want to scream. "I'm going to kill that piece of crap!!"

"Oh Amber. We'll fix this. Tristan's a good guy. Daniel's a douche. Come on. Let's go back right now and talk to Tristan."

"How can I face him right now, Aria?"

"I know it's hard Amber. But if you ignore him, then he might believe that you kissed Daniel, not the other way around."

"Yeah, I guess you're right. Let's go."

Hey guys! Today is Remembrance Day or Veteran's Day, whatever you call it. In Canada it's Remembrance Day.

Anyway, I updated! Quickly! I'm awesome. Anyway, I think updates are going to be quicker and longer now, because I'm getting really excited about this book. We're nearing the climax, and that makes me excited. (I'm not making promises about when the next update will be)

So, in the last chapter, correctly figured out the age of the girls drawn in 2050.   also got it right, but there may have been some cheating

Thanks to anyone who comments and votes, it makes me so happy. Thank you so much, I love you guys!

Jen

(I feel like Daniel's going to be getting lots of hate comments)

18

I hate Daniel.

So much.

What did I ever do to him?

Um Amber? That inner voice in my head asks me. You did choose Tristan over him. Well yeah, but he can go after Zoe or something. The two of us just aren't the same as me and Tristan.

UGH!!

I hate him!

Everything was finally getting good, and then Daniel had to go and screw it all up.

Aria and I head back to where Tristan and Quinn are sitting, having a conversation written on a piece of paper.

Aria and I sit down, Aria back to beside Quinn. Me, I sit kind of outside of the group. Both Tristan and Quinn are glaring at me, so I know I shouldn't push my luck.

"Tristan, I-"

He cuts me off. "Aria, please tell her that I don't want to talk to her."

"But," Aria protests in my defense. "She can explain. It wasn't her! It was Dan-"

"I don't care! I refuse to talk to her!"

I know that seeing that hurt him, but know Tristan's hurting me. And I hate it. Stupid Daniel.

Aria sighs in defeat. "Amber? Uhhh. He doesn't want to talk to you." She trails off at the end.

+++

I must have fallen asleep, because I'm jolted awake when the bell rings. The bell! Maybe we're no longer trapped in here!

Everyone springs up and runs to the doors to our dorms. Some older guy that I don't know tries the door.

"Nope," he says, the excitement drained from is face. Others go try the door handle, and it is indeed locked.

Lee claps her hands. "Guys!" she yells, trying to get our attention. We all look over to her and quiet down. "We should look around. Just because the doors didn't open, that bell could mean something else."

Everyone choruses different versions of "Good idea Lee."

We all start looking around the common room. After about five minutes, someone shouts out.

"Guys! I found something."

We all crowd around.

"It's food!" one of the guys screams. "Hallelujah!"

After some commotion, Lee and a few others get everyone's attention.

"Okay," one of the guys with Lee says. "It's true, we have food." A cheer goes up. "There's enough for everyone, but its not a lot."

"So, I know you're all hungry," Lee says, "But Dominic, Brianne, Corey and I think that we need some organization here. Who knows how long this will be going on for. So, we want to have two people, preferably a guy and a girl, representing each age group. We'll let each age vote for the leader people. The four of us are going 'run' for our age groups, but if we aren't selected, we'll back down."

The other girl, Brianne, I'm assuming, speaks up. "We'll start with the youngest. Any 15-year-old interested in doing whatever this is, come up here."

Zoe springs up and rushes to the front as her posse chants "Zoe! Zoe! Zoe!"

Dave and Daniel both go up, as well as Nerdboy, or Zach, whichever you prefer. Duckface heads up to the front.

"Aria," I hiss. "You should go up."

"Heck no! You three would be my only votes! No one knows me!"

"But look at the other options!" I insist.

"Then you go!" She says. "You have a way better chance than me."

"Are you sure?" I ask uncertainly.

"Go." she urges.

Slowly, I stand up and head to the front, at the same time as Tess.

I stop abruptly. "No," I say. "Not against Tess."

"Amber you have to. You're the only good one."

Quinn nods, and I think I even see Tristan nod, just a little bit.

I breathe out. "Okay."

I head up to the front and join Zoe, Daniel, Duckface, Nerdboy and Dave.

"Anyone else?" Lee asks.

No one responds.

"I'll take that as a no," one of the two guys, either Corey or Dominic, says. "Let's start with the guys. Introduce yourselves please."

"I guess I'll start," says Nerdboy in his nasal voice. He pushes up his glasses. "I'm Zach."

"I'm Daniel. Vote for me!" He shouts, and does jazz hands.

"Dave."

"We're not having ballots or anything, so raise your hand if you're 15 and wanna vote for Zach," says Lee.

They count Zach's votes.

"Okay, now votes for Dave."

I raise my hand. He's a good leader.

"And last, Daniel." Then hands go up.

I am really anxious to know who it is. If it's Daniel then I'm sitting back down.

"Alright," Brianne says. "We have Dave, with eleven votes, Daniel with seven and Zach with three votes. Dave, you can stay up here, and Daniel and Zach, you can go and sit down. Now for the girls. Introduce yourselves please."

"I'm Zoe, and I'm going to win."

"I'm Erica."

"The name's Tess," she says exuberantly, and strikes a pose.

"And I'm Amber."

We go through the same voting process as we did with the guys. In the end, I have five votes, Duckface has three, Zoe has five and Tess has seven. I head back to Aria and the guys.

"You were close, Amber." Then she leans in close and whispers, "Tristan voted for you."

In the other age groups no one else wants to help lead this, so Lee, and one of the guys that was with her, Dominic, is his name, are representing the 17 year olds, and Brianne and Corey representing the 19 year olds. This whole election seems kind of pointless to me, why didn't the four of them just take charge?

They leader people all gather together and soon enough they're handing out granola bars, apples, oranges, bananas and water.

Everyone is happy to have food, and it immediately boosts the morale.

Aria and I play all sorts of random games, but eventually she wants some time with Quinn.

The chatter starts to die down, and we are all getting sleepy. Tristan is the first of our corner to fall asleep. Aria and Quinn drift off leaning on each other shortly afterward. But I am left with my thoughts, not able to fall asleep.

+++

This really is all my fault, isn't it? I wanted to come here so badly, and now I've screwed everything up. I hurt Tristan. If only I hadn't gone with Daniel. Then maybe Tristan and I would look the way Aria and Quinn do right now. But no. I had to screw it all up. I'm a failure. I ruined it all.

+++

"Amber? Are you okay?"

I open my eyes and see Tristan. Why is my face all wet? Wait, was I crying?

"Amber?" He asks again, cautiously.

"Sorry, what?"

"Are you okay? You were crying."

"Yeah-I. I-uh," I stutter. "Can we talk?"

He replies softly, "Yes."

"Tristan, I-I'm really really sorry. You didn't deserve any of this. I'll apologize for everything. But you have to believe that I didn't kiss him back, nor did I want to kiss him. I swear. If you don't believe me, I can just exit your life. But please, please believe me. I really like you Tristan. I never meant to hurt you. I only went to talk to Daniel because I thought if I talked to him one last time I could make him stay away. And he is going to stay away, he just wanted to ruin everything first." I stop, out of breath.

"I believe you Amber. I promise I wasn't ignoring you, there was just a voice in my head that kept repeating. What if she did kiss him? What if she likes him? And I was worried that that voice would be right. I just needed to regain my sanity before I talked to you. But I trust you Amber, I really do." He pauses. "And I hate seeing you sad or scared, waking up from a nightmare like that."

I think I have tears in my eyes. What did I do to deserve this?

"Tristan," I say. "I don't know what I did to deserve such an amazing person like you, but I promise, I never want to hurt you again."

"Amber, I really like you. And like I said, I trust you. But let's go back to sleep now, okay?"

We head back to the corner and sit down by Aria and Quinn. He puts his arm around me and pulls me close to him.

I quickly fall into a deep, nightmare free sleep.

+++

YAY! CHAPTER 18!!!! Sorry you guys had to wait so long, thanks for being patient.

Thank you so much to everyone who faithfully reads, comments and votes. It means so much to me. Love you guys!

Anyway, hope you like the chapter. I'm gonna be pretty busy the next few weeks with choir, but I'll try and do another update in the near future.

Jen

19

P LEASE TELL ME WHAT YOU THINK OF THE NEW COVER!

It's been a week since Tristan and I made up.

We got back into the dorms a couple days ago, and things are returning to normal. Well, as normal as they've every been here.

"Amber!" Aria calls from outside of Tess's and my room.

"What?"

"Come here!"

I get up and meet her outside of my dorm. "What?" I ask.

"There's a group of people going to play paintball," she says. "The boys are going and they want us to come. Do you want to come?"

"Meh. I don't know. Are you going?"

"If you're going, I am," Aria tells me. "So make a decision."

"Aria! I don't know! Why are you making me make the decision?"

"Oh is Amber a chicken?" Aria teases. "Come on," she says, grabbing my arm. "Let's go."

Aria drags me through the hallways, past the common room and to the playing field outside. I've never been out here before. There are a whole bunch of people gathered around out here. Tristan and Quinn widen the circle so we can join.

I look around the circle. There's me, Aria, Tristan, Quinn, Tess, Ethyn, Oliver, some other random guys, and of course, just my luck, Daniel and Cody.

"Aria I don't know if I can be here with them."

"We'll make sure we're not on their team so that we can shoot them a lot," Tristan reassures me.

I nod. "Okay."

"Guys!" Oliver calls out. "We need two captains. Who wants to be a captain?"

Cody, Daniel and Tess all say that they want to be captain.

"Guys," I hiss. "I don't want to be on any of those teams!"

"Same," Aria says.

"Only two of them will be captains," Tristan reminds.

"Let's let Tess be one of the captains. Daniel and Cody, rock paper scissors." Oliver says.

The two compete, and Cody wins. Then him and Tess play for first pick.

Cody wins again and chooses Daniel.

Not surprisingly, Tess chooses Oliver. She must still like him. Cody's next pick is Ethyn. Aria, Quinn and I will probably be last.

But much to my surprise, the name Tess calls as her next pick is mine.

I'm so confused. Aria gives me a little shove and I head over. Tess hands me a paintball gun and a mask.

"Thanks," I say. "But why'd you choose me?"

She just shrugs in response. "Do you want Tristan here too?"

Wow. Is she being nice?

I nod in response to her question.

Pretty soon the teams are made. Over here on team Tess, we have Oliver, me, Tristan, and a guy who introduces himself as Troy and Quinn.

Cody's team has Daniel, Ethyn, Aria, and two other guys.

"Poor Aria," I say to Tristan and Quinn.

They nod in agreement.

Tess and Cody have decided to play capture the flag. Each team gets one doctor.

Tess comes back and we get right down to business. "Okay. We're going to make a great strategy guys. I want to make partners for our team. So Troy and Quinn, you guys are going to be on defense. Shoot anyone who comes near the flag. Amber and Tristan, I want you guys to stay near the center line and save our team from the jail. Oliver, me and you are going to be on offense. Got it guys?"

"Okay, but what are me and Amber supposed to be doing, other than saving our team? What do we do when no one's in jail?"

"Just play either defense or offense, whatever you see fit," Tess tells us.

"Alright."

"Sounds good," I say.

"Cody!" Tess yells. "Are you goons ready?"

Cody scoffs. "You won't be calling us goons after you've lost!"

"As if that will happen," Tess laughs.

"Let's do this!"

Our two teams head to our respective sides of the fields. There is already a rope marking the center, and a jail outlined. I guess field isn't the right word for it. This place reminds of the camp I used to go to back home, where we played capture the flag, without paintball guns, in the ravine. There are trees, and hills, and it will be perfect.

"The boundaries are marked with neon green flags," Tess tells us.

Troy ties our flag to a tree branch, and we walk to the center line, as the other team does the same thing.

"Ready?" Tristan asks me.

"Not really. I've played capture the flag before, but I've never shot a paintball gun. Does getting shot hurt?"

"Not really. It just stings a bit at first. But when we're on our side they can't shoot us. So it'll be Tess and Oliver getting shot at mostly."

Tess and Cody shake hands, and then the game starts. "Amber, stay close to the line," Tristan shouts over the wild screaming. "Shoot them once they come onto our side!"

With that, he disappears into the brush. I've never even shot a paintball gun before. How am I supposed to do this.

"Amber!" Tess screams at me. "Quit standing around! Do something! Get in the game!"

Oops. Guess I stood around for too long.

Where's Tristan?

Just as the thought crosses my mind, Cody, Daniel, Ethyn and the two other guys come sprinting across the line.

I hear Tristan shout, "Defenders! They're coming!"

In the chaos of six people storming our side, I see Oliver and Tess sneaking into enemy territory.

Then I remember what I'm supposed to do. Tristan has already shot Daniel, and Ethyn turned back. Quinn takes a shot at Cody and hits him. But where are the other two?

"Amber! Look behind you!"

I turn around and blindly pull the trigger a few times.

When I stop shooting, I hear my team cheering for me.

"You managed to get both of them Amber!"

Moments later, Tess and Oliver are sprinting towards our side with the other team's flag. Ethyn is shooting at them, and Aria is struggling with her gun. The other four are of no help, because we have them in jail.

I scream and cheer for them to run, and it works. Tess crosses the line with their flag, beaming.

Cody grunts. "You win this one. Let's play again."

"You want to get creamed again?"

"No, I want to win."

We give them their flag back, and we start again. It starts slower this time, and I have a better idea of what to do.

This time I'm going hide like Tristan did, and be a secret assassin, instead of the obvious one I was last time.

I jog around the huge dip in the ground to get to a patch of bushes. I hear some yells, so I go a little faster.

All of a sudden something slams into me. I tumble down the hill, and everything goes black.

Dun dun dun!

You must all hate me. Mwahahaha! I love cliffhangers.

I have three more days until Christmas break! That should mean updates! Yay!

You may have noticed that I changed the cover. PLEASE TELL ME WHAT YOU THINK.

Anyway, vote and comment like usual, I love you guys

Jen

+20+

∧ ^^^ Up there is my favourite Christmas ornament: bookworm Jen.

The first thing I hear is Tristan's voice. The world around me is still dark, but I can hear him speaking.

"Is she awake yet?"

"No," I hear Aria say. "I'm starting to get worried."

I can hear you! Aria! Tristan! I can hear you!

"Do you think we should get help?" Asks Tristan.

"I don't know. There must be an infirmary around here some-where, but I don't know what they'd do there. What do you think?"

"I don't know. There is an infirmary, I know that. For the most part it's run by older people, like Greyson and Jay. Maybe I could find out who's working there today?"

Aria seems to like this idea. "Yeah, that would be good."

I feel the little bit of consciousness that I have slipping away.

Aria continued her thought. "I think that maybe-"

The hands of sleep pull me back under.

This time I really wake up. My eyes are open and I can lift my head. I decide that they must have brought me to the infirmary, because this is most definitely not my room.

I sit up and look around. I'm so tired, and I really don't know why. The door opens and I turn my head to look over there.

"Amber!" Aria exclaims. "You're awake!"

I try to say yes, but my throat is so dry that I can't make a sound. So I just nod.

"Amber?" She asks again.

I nod again.

"Oh! Do you need some water?"

I nod a third time.

"Okay. I'll be right back." Aria dashes out of the room and returns shortly with a glass of water.

I gratefully accept the glass of water and take a few sips before asking, in a still hoarse voice, "What's going on?"

"What do you remember?" Aria asks me.

"I remember being outside, then there's a big blank space from there to when I overheard you and Tristan having a conversation about taking me to the infirmary. And I'm assuming that that's where we are now?"

"Yeah. We talked to Mitchel and Kendra and they know the girl that's here today."

I nod. "What happened to me? I don't remember."

"I'll go get Tristan," Aria tells me, "And we'll explain together."

Aria leaves the room again, and I take this time to get comfortable. I push myself up into a sitting position, and everything hurts.

I groan in pain and reach for my water.

Aria comes back into the room with Tristan and Quinn.

"Amber!" Tristan exclaims. "I'm so glad you're okay!"

I smile, glad I have friends who care about me.

"Can you guys please explain what happened?" I ask impatiently.

"Yeah, yeah, don't get all anxious," Aria says with a laugh. "No, I'm kidding. We were out playing paintball, and then one of the guys from the other team slammed into you, and you fell down the big dip in the ground. Then-"

Aria is cut off by a girl opening the door.

"Hey June," Tristan says, greeting her.

I'm confused.

"Amber this is June, she's one of the ones that works in the infirmary right now," Aria tells me.

"Yep," June says. "The ADCCG just sends me what I need and notes of what to do with it. So I have some painkillers for you." She hands me two small white pills and a Dixie cup of water.

I swallow the pills and thank her.

"Not a problem. We also did some x-rays, nothing is broken, but you have a pretty nasty sprain on your ankle and you're pretty bruised up."

"Will I be on crutches, or what?" I ask.

We have crutches that you can use, but you should only need them for the first few days. I'll wrap your ankle with a tensor bandage when you leave."

"Okay," I say, overloaded with all this information. "Thanks."

"Not a problem. I'm glad you're awake," June tells me and leaves the room.

"Anyway," Tristan says. "Back to the story. So Cody was the one to body check you, but Daniel had a part in planning it. So a whole bunch of people ran down the hill and we carried you back to your dorm, unconscious. The next day, you still weren't awake, so Aria and I debated taking you here. As you can-"

I interrupt. "I heard that conversation."

"So we brought you here. That was yesterday. So you were out for all of yesterday, half of the day before, and half of today."

I take a moment to digest the new information.

"Can I leave now?"

"I'll go ask June," Aria says, and drags Quinn with her.

Tristan sits down on the edge of my bed. "I was really worried."

I nod, not knowing what to say.

A few minutes later Aria and Quinn come back with June in tow.

"Ready to get out of here?" June asks me.

"Yes."

"Okay. I have a tensor bandage here to wrap up your ankle, so let's do that. There are crutches in the corner of the main room, could one of you go and get them?" She asks the others.

Quinn heads out to get them.

My friends help me sit up and June does a great job of wrapping up my ankle. Quinn returns with my crutches just as June finishes.

"Our jobs are being switched soon, but Amber, you can always come back for painkillers."

"Okay. Thanks again June."

"It's not a problem," she tells me with a smile.

I slowly stand up off the bed and Tristan hands me my crutches.

Aria and Quinn head out the door, and Tristan and I follow.

"You good?"

"Yeah. It's kinda hard, but I can do it."

"I hate to tell you this, but we're in the basement. There's a lot of steep stairs up here."

I groan. "Why!"

Tristan laughs. "So dramatic."

Aria and Quinn are waiting at the base of the stairs.

"Give them your crutches," Tristan tells me.

"But-why?"

"You have to get up these stairs somehow."

"And I'll need my crutches or do it, numbskull."

"Just give them your crutches and trust me."

I reluctantly hand over the crutches and Tristan picks me up bridal style.

I squeal. "Tristan! Put me down!"

He laughs. "You have to get up the stairs somehow!"

"Oh my gosh, please don't drop me!"

"Do you really not trust me? You can go up these four flights of stairs on crutches, or I can carry you."

I relent. "You're right."

"Well of course I am," he says with a smug smile.

I laugh and he heads up the stairs.

When we reach the top, I can tell Tristan's tired, but he won't admit it. Aria and Quinn hand me my crutches.

The four of us go to the common room for a while, and then go to lunch. For lunch there's pasta salad. I don't realize it until now, but I'm really hungry.

"Amber, we can get you food," Aria tells me.

"Yeah, just go sit down at our table," Tristan adds.

"Thanks."

I crutch over to our table, feeling like all eyes are on me. This sucks.

Tristan, Aria and Quinn come sit down and we eat our lunch in peace. Afterwards we go to class, where we do some crap with polynomials.

Right before curfew, Tristan and I go downstairs to get me painkillers. Again, he refuses to let me use my crutches.

+++

It's been five days since I woke up. Today I'm going without my crutches.

I'm not sure why I'm awake at 5:00am, but I am.

"Psssst. Amber!" I sit up abruptly and look to see Aria and Kendra at the door. "Get up!" They whisper.

I pull some sweats and a hoodie over what I'm already wearing and sneak out the door.

"What's going on?" I ask quietly.

"Mitchel came to my room and got me up," Kendra says. "Jay and Greyson want to have a meeting."

The three of us head down the hallway in the dark, and I struggle a bit.

"Oh! Right! Sorry Amber!" Aria apologizes. She takes my arm and let's me lean on her a bit. I still have the bandage on my ankle giving me a little bit of support.

We go to what I think is the same storage closet we usually meet in. Tristan, Quinn, Mitchel, Jay and Greyson are already waiting.

Greyson stands up and hugs me. "What did you do?" He asks, sounding really concerned when he sees my ankle.

"I sprained it. I'm off of the crutches now, so I get to limp around."

"Who told you to stop using the crutches? How long has it been?"

"June was working in the infirmary. She said I only needed them for five days."

"It's never going to heal like that! The ADCCG dumb-"

"Greyson! Calm down," Kendra interrupts.

"No! They don't want her ankle to be completely healed! That's why we're here!"

"What's going on?" I ask.

Jay pipes up, ready to explain. "The reason we're here is because we want to escape. The job rotations were switched again yesterday, and Greyson and I are finally on security. It's time to get out of here."

+++

Bam! I bet none of you expected that!

Anyway, I'm super happy that it's winter break now and I can relax.
Hopefully there will be another update soon.

Don't forget to comment and vote!

Jen

-21-

Hey friends! I'm so so so so so so so so so so so so sorry that it took me almost a month to update! But without further ado, here's chapter 21!

"Escape?" Tristan asks in disbelief.

"Yes," Jay says, nodding confirmation. "It's been in the works for a while."

Greyson pipes up. "When Mitchel told me that Amber was here, we had to include you guys. What kind of big brother would be be if I left my baby sister and her friends in this awful place?"

There is a break and the conversation as we absorb this new information.

Timidly, Aria asks the question I was afraid to ask. "Has anyone escaped from here before?"

"Not that we know of," Kendra tells us. "But there's also no record of anyone trying to escape."

"I guess that's mildly comforting," I mutter under my breath.

"How long has this been being planned for?" Tristan asks.

"Greyson and Jay have been planning for quite a while. Then Mitch and I got on board and started to help. After we were locked out of the dorms we knew we had to put the plan into action as soon as possible."

Tristan nods.

Aria is conversing with Quinn. I assume he's asking her to say something for him.

"Quinn was wondering if we get to know about this plan? Or will we just blindly do as we're told?"

"You make it sound like we're using you as pawns," Mitchel says with a laugh. He looks to Greyson, who speaks up to answer the question.

"Really though, the four of us know the whole plan. We only told those two lovebirds," he gestures to Mitchel and Kendra. To prove the point Mitch leans over and kisses Kendra on the cheek. "We only told them everything recently," he continues. "We'll tell you guys most parts, but we decided that until we're gone, it's better if fewer people know."

"Not that we don't trust you guys or anything!" Jay adds hastily.

I nod. "It's not offending, it makes sense. Can you tell us the basics?"

"Of course," Greyson tells me with a smile. "So, as we said before, it was time for a job rotation. The jobs are working in the infirmary, as you would have seen, security, janitor stuff and other miscellaneous things like that. Jay and I finally got put on security with a couple other guys that we're friends with. They're trustworthy. We're planning to leave in the night. Once we've decided on a day, we're going to tell them. They think that Jay wants to go to one of the girls dorms and, you know," he pauses. "I think you guys know what I'm getting at. You're not that young. So those guys are going to blow a circuit, causing the breaker to trip. That way the ADCCG can't put blame on anyone but an electrician."

"That's really smart," Tristan praises.

"We've been thinking for a while."

Jay takes over with explaining the plan. "So we'll leave in the night, when the all the security cameras are off. Then we'll figure out where we are, and go from there."

Greyson buts in, clearly not happy with the way his friend is explaining. "He makes it sound unorganized, but I promise it's not."

"That's such a lie!" Jay complains.

"No it's not."

"You're such a boob! Amber, your brother is a boob."

"Okay, okay," Kendra says in effort to shut them up. Clearly she's used to playing peacekeeper.

"You guys have any questions?" Greyson asks. "See Jay! I'm not a boob, I'm nice."

"Yeah yeah yeah, shut up ya idiots," Kendra says passively.

"But really," Mitch says. "Do you guys have questions? I might be able to answer them, cause those two are a little busy arguing over who's a bigger boob," he says with a laugh.

"Who put them in charge?" Kendra mutters under her breath.

Mitch gives her a soft kiss. "You know it'll work out, babe," he whispers.

"But what if it doesn't?"

"It will."

Aria and Quinn are talking quietly, and Tristan and I are sitting here awkwardly, watching the romantic exchange, and the immature exchange.

"How's your ankle?" Tristan asks me.

"Not good. It's been sore the past few days, but walking on it has made it swell up again."

He puts an arm around me. I smile and lean against his broad shoulder. But of course, he has to ruin the moment. "Can I see your ankle?"

"Yeah, sure."

I take off my sock, and roll up my sweatpants.

"Amber! It's really swollen!"

And of course Greyson overhears. Here comes the overprotective brother. "Amber, lemme see your ankle."

I gesture to my ankle. "Right there, free viewing, no admission fees," I mutter sarcastically.

"Shut up. Amber, you need to be on crutches. I think we're done here," Greyson says, taking charge once again.

"I can carry Amber back to the dorms," Tristan says.

"She needs to use the crutches as much as possible, but the AD-CCG will try not to let her. They usually want us to be minimally healed, so we'll have permanent limps and whatnot."

Tristan nods. Then they tell us that Mitch and Kendra will come and get us next time we're needed. Aria and Quinn head out and Tristan picks me up and follows.

"What time is it?" I ask.

Aria looks at the clock. "Wow, crap! It's already seven!"

"Well, we did meet at five in the morning."

"True. But there are probably people in the common room," Aria says. "Everyone's awake."

Tristan thinks for a second. "How about you go get Amber's crutches from her room? And we'll wait in the common room. Cause they aren't going to let me come in the girls dorms."

Aria nods. Tristan puts me down and we open the doors to the common room. Tristan, Quinn and I head to the closest couch, me in a lot of pain. "Sorry," Tristan whispers. "I didn't think you would want people to see me carrying you."

"Probably a good idea. If anyone asks, we'll say we took me to the infirmary early in the morning."

He nods.

The clock on my bedside table reads 4:28am. I've rewrapped my ankle six trillion times. I had three doses of pain pills throughout the day, and one right before bed. I should be sound asleep. I have to be awake in two and a half hours. But I can't shake this freaking insomnia. My ankle hurts, and my head is going crazy thinking about the plan.

Do I want to escape?

Of course you do Amber! You'd be crazy not to!

But I don't know what lies outside these walls.

Do you want to be here alone? Away from Tristan? Aria and Quinn? Greyson? Amber! You could see Ty again!

But I'm scared.

You're brave, Amber. You can do this.

YAY! I updated! I'm really sorry it didn't come sooner. I have exams next week and the week after, so don't expect an update. (I have to write FIVE exams, and a choir exam!!!!!!!!!)

I want to talk about the picture at the top. I've also put it on the cover of 2056. #writteninaction is a campaign to promote books other than teen fiction, ect. Check out the profile: for more info.

Don't forget to vote and comment!

jen

E scape. It's all that's been on my mind since our meeting three days ago.

We headed to the common room after finishing dinner - barbecue chicken and potatoes.

I'm still on crutches, which really sucks. I can only hope that I can be off them before we go. I can limo around without them, but the pain is awful. Kind of like right now, even though I'm sitting.

"Tristan," I whisper, trying not to interrupt the conversation with Aria, Quinn, Kendra and Mitch. "I need pain pills."

"'Kay. Let's go. We'll be right back," he tells them.

"Where're you going?"

"Infirmary," he says, nodding his head at me.

We head out of the common room and I have an urge to take his hand. But of course my hands are occupied by these stupid crutches. Stupid Cody and Daniel.

Tristan helps me down the stairs as usual. He's so good to me. I'm so lucky.

And then he puts me down at the bottom of the stairs and catches me starting at him.

"Whatcha looking at there Amber?"

I blush. Why me?

"Nothing."

"Mmmhmm," he nods. "I bet that's it. It couldn't have been that you were looking at this face. Nope. Definitely not," he shakes his head, laughing at me.

I blush and giggle. "Why would I be looking at your face?"

"Hmmm. Maybe cause you're hopelessly in love with me?" He says teasingly.

I stick my tongue out at him. Childish, I know.

"So mature," he says with a grin.

I just stick my tongue out again, and crutch down the hallway toward the infirmary.

Tristan catches up with me, which isn't very hard, considering the fact that I'm on crutches.

He opens the door to the infirmary for me and the guy inside greets us.

"Hi! I'm Colin! Can I help you out?"

"Yeah, Amber here is on crutches," Tristan says, sounding a little annoyed if I'm not mistaken. "She needs some pain meds."

"Okay," Colin says, opening a filing cabinet. "Amber..." He flips through some folders. "What year are you from?"

"Twenty fifty-six."

"Province?"

"Manitoba."

He flips through a few more folders. "Ah, here we are. Amber Matlock, Manitoba, Twenty fifty-six. It says here Amber that you were supposed to be off of your crutches three days ago."

"Yes, but I cannot walk on my ankle. Three days ago when I didn't use crutches it swelled like a balloon. The other girl that's been here just gives me pain pills - no questions asked."

The infirmary dude eases my crutches away from me. I wince in pain as weight is put onto my left ankle. I quickly shift my weight to my right side and Tristan is quick to put my arm across him for some support.

"Just give her some meds and her crutches!" Tristan shouts at Colin.

"The official ADCCG file is kept up to date and gives precise instructions for what we need to do here. You can look at the file if you like. It says right here that she should not be on crutches. I can give you some pain pills though Amber."

Tristan throws up his arms in frustration.

Colin hands me a couple painkillers and some water. I swallow them.

"Come on Tristan. Let's go."

"But you need your crutches!"

I sigh. Clearly neither of the two are going to relent anytime soon.

Tristan argues with Colin for a while longer about giving me crutches back. Eventually they reach a compromise: Colin will switch my tensor bandage for a stronger brace splint thing. I'm not entirely sure what it is, but it gives my ankle a lot more support. But Tristan still won't let me walk up the stairs on my own.

+++

I got my brace last night, and this morning I'm going back to the infirmary. I'm supposed to get pain pills and whoever's there will adjust the brace.

Even though I say I can go alone, Tristan comes with me.

"Let me go down the stairs Tristan. The brace really helps, and in gonna need to be able to walk for the plan."

He sighs. "I guess you're right."

"I always am," I say, sticking out my tongue. "I can hobble around. Don't worry."

I get my brace adjusted and take the pain pills in record time. It's a different girl there this time - thankfully not Colin.

The girl tells me that I'm being cut off from the pain pills. Guess I'll just have to suck it up.

When Tristan and I get upstairs to the common room, Aria and Quinn are talking with Mitch and Kendra. We head over to join them.

"How's that ankle?" Kendra asks me.

"It's alright. The brace is working well."

"You can walk on it okay?" Mitch asks.

"Yeah. I'm a little slow, but yeah."

"Okay, good. Because Greyson told his friends that Jay is 'going to see a girl tonight,'" he says, making air quotes.

I nod.

Wow. Tonight is the night we leave this place. It's still hard to believe that we're actually escaping.

+++

We go through our day as usual. A gym class in which we run laps the whole time - I walked laps to get used to using my ankle, we do math worksheets and have meals.

Kendra and Mitch catch up with us again in the evening.

They explain the plan for this evening. "Greyson and Jay pulled some strings so that your roommates have stuff to do this evening. There are backpacks in each of your closets. Fill them with warm, practical clothes and other things you might need. Nothing frivolous. Greyson has a first aid kit with him. Your roommates are having a sleepover with some of the older people and some your age. Girls, spend the night in Aria's room, guys in Tristan's. Got it?"

"Yep."

"We'll come and get you," Kendra adds to what Mitch just told us.

We all head back to our rooms to pack.

Aria and I start in my room, because we're spending the night in her room.

I pack t shirts, tights, sweats, long sleeves, and a fleece hoodie in my bag. I leave out a sports bra, black long sleeve athletic shirt and black tights to put on later. Then we head to Aria's room. She packs very similarly to me.

The two of us go through the motions of getting ready for bed. Before we get under the covers, we get dressed in the clothes that we left out of our backpacks.

We get dressed and lie in our beds. I doze off for a while, but the anticipation is making it hard to sleep.

At 2:38am Kendra sneaks into our room.

"Come on girls. It's time."

We steal out of the dorms and meet up with Mitch, Quinn and Tristan. Everyone is very quiet.

"Ready?" Mitch asks.

Moments later, the doors to the common room open. Jay and Greyson appear, and motion for us to follow. Very quietly, we do just that. Tristan stays right beside me, probably still worried that I can't walk.

After twists and turns through unfamiliar hallways, we reach a large metal door.

Greyson unlocks it, using some sort of mechanism that I don't recognize.

The door swings open, and the reality hits me. We've done it. But we aren't in the clear yet.

It's cold outside, and I wish I had worn my fleece, instead of packing it. Oh well. It's too late now.

We walk for about an hour until we reach a very brick wall of about fifteen feet with menacing coils of barbed wire on top.

Uh-oh.

But Greyson and Jay must have been expecting this. Jay pulls a homemade rope ladder from his bag, and I realize that they have much bigger backpacks than us. The six of us have standard school sized backpacks. They have 'live out of this backpack for a year' size backpacks.

The boys work together to get the ladder hooked on the top of the barbed wire. It's decided that Jay will got first, and Greyson last.

Slowly but surely, as we all hold our breath, Jay climbs the wall. He pulls the ladder so that half of it is on our side, and half hangs down his side so he can climb down. Greyson holds our side of the ladder so it doesn't slip.

Kendra goes, then Mitch, then Tristan, and then it's my turn. I know that my brother is holding the ladder, and Tristan is waiting for me on the other side.

I climb over the barbed wire and start my descent. I'm a little slower than the others due to my ankle.

I Mitch, Kendra and Tristan, who are crouched down in a ditch that runs along this side of the wall. Jay is holding the ladder.

Once everyone is on the non ADCCG side of the wall, were pretty happy. We've been gone for about two hours so it's about 4:40am. It's still dark.

"We want to get as far as we can in the dark, okay guys? We're going to start walking now," Jay announces.

Tristan comes to walk beside me, and has me put my arm around him to make it easier for me to walk. Greyson and Jay are speaking in hushed tones, Mitch and Kendra are holding hands, Aria and Quinn are walking together in silence, and Tristan and I are just absorbing the fact that we've escaped.

Another hour later we take a quick break. Some protein bars are passed around and we keep going.

The sun is beginning to rise, and Jay announces that it's nearly eight o'clock in the morning.

We've been walking across a barren plain for the last few hours and we reach some trees and take a break.

I sit down to rest my ankle, and Tristan sits down beside me and takes my hand in his.

Everyone is sitting down, enjoying the fresh air, when we hear a gun shot. We scramble for our things and run. Tristan takes my backpack to make running a little easier for me.

A few more shots ring out. But we're literally the only people in sight.

We slow our run to a jog, and then to a walk.

"I don't know where those were coming from," Greyson says, trying to mask his worry.

We continue walking. There is a thick forest way ahead in the distance. It'll probably be a good place to hide.

"Let's aim to get there by midday," Mitch says.

+++

It's only been about fifteen minutes since we regrouped after hearing those gun shots. But I'm going to guess that they came from the helicopters that are overhead.

Before we can talk about the fact that there are what appear to be government helicopters above us, they open fire.

We sprint. Running for the cover of the forest, we are concerned only about each other's safety. Tristan isn't able to grab my backpack this time, but he grabs my arm and makes sure I'm right beside him.

At first it's just a few warning shots.

Then I see Aria fall. Quinn helps her up and tries to keep moving, but she collapses a few feet from where she first fell.

She's been shot.

Quinn bends over her, tries to help her, so they can keep moving. But it's no use.

"Aria!" I scream. "No!"

"C'mon Amber!" Tristan says. "We have to keep going. I can't let you get shot."

"But-but-"

I look back. Quinn is sitting with Aria in his lap, crying, holding the girl he loved.

He motions for us to keep going. To leave them.

I cast one last glance back and follow Tristan.

They're gone.

+++

Ohmygosh ohmygosh ohmygosh what have I done??

I need to thank you guys so much for your continuous support of this story. A few days ago twenty fifty six reached #43 in science fiction. I never imagined that this book would make it so far. Thank you so much guys.

Jen <3

PS-that's my bookshelf at the top. I made it into a rainbow.

Hey guys. I'm sorry I went so long without an update. Please read the author's note at the end of the chapter.

It's dark in our cave now, and we're finally safe.

But I can't stop replaying the events of the day through my head. The day haunts me.

We ran for a really long time. My ankle is absolutely killing me.

When I was to distracted by leaving Quinn and Aria to die, Tristan pulled me along to safety. The bullets ceased for a bit, and in those precious moments, we got organized. Tristan told the other four what had happened. Mitch and Kendra took my backpack and Tristan's backpack, and Tristan picked me up. I just couldn't run anymore, and he could tell.

We started running again, me on Tristan's back and we tried to put as much distance as we could between us and the government helicopters.

They came back soon enough, armed with more bullets. We were really close to the forest at that point, so we ran as fast as we could.

Under the shelter of the trees we caught our breath. I was out of breath too, not from running, but because I was terrified. Tristan took his backpack and mine from Kendra and Mitch, and we walked through the forest.

We found this cave just as it was beginning to get dark. I was shivering, just like I was early in the morning, because I stupidly left my fleece in my bag. Jay checked out the entire cave with a flashlight, making sure that nobody and nothing was in it.

We put our bags in there, and I collapse to the ground. The exhaustion, hunger and pain had caught up to me. Tristan sits down beside me, holding me. Jay and Greyson go look for some fire wood, while Mitch and Kendra take inventory of the supplies in our backpacks.

Now that we've stopped, my mind goes straight to Aria and Quinn.

"Tristan. They're-th-they're gone," I say through my tears.

"I know, Amber."

It's then that I realize that Tristan is in as much pain as I am. I wrap my arms around him, and we hold each other, my face is buried in his shoulder.

"Amber, you're freezing cold! You're shaking!" Tristan exclaims. "Kendra, can you pass me her fleece?"

"Yeah, of course. How's your ankle doing Amber?"

"I don't know."

"We should probably check it out," she says.

"Greyson will want to see too," Mitch tells Kendra. "Let's wait a bit."

I pull on my warm fleece hoodie, and immediately relish in the extra warmth.

Tristan wraps his arms around me again to keep me warm. I don't know what I'd do without him.

Greyson and Jay return with some wood to make a small fire.

Mitch passes them a pack of matches, and once we have rocks set around the wood so the fire doesn't spread, they light the fire.

The light and warmth greatly helps increase the morale in the cave.

"How's your ankle Amber?" My brother asks me.

"I don't know."

"Does it hurt?"

"It did. I've kinda gotten used to the pain."

"Amber!" Greyson throws his arms up in frustration. "Do you want to be able to walk again?"

"Greyson, I was just trying to get to safety. Would you rather I be like-li-like Aria and Quinn?" I scream.

"Shhh, shhh," Tristan whispers to be. "Amber. You're okay. Calm down now, please?"

I buried my face in Tristan's shoulder. I just want all of this to go away! Why did they have to die? It's just not fair!

After a while, I've consoled myself. I don't know what I'd do if Tristan was gone too.

"Amber," Greyson says gently. "I'm so, so sorry." He wraps me in a hug. "I didn't mean to make you cry, I'm just worried about you. You're my little sister; I don't want to see you hurting."

I hug him back. "Thank you."

"I love you Amber. I'll always be here for you."

"I love you too, big brother."

Tristan and I are sitting together at the back of the cave with one of our blankets. The others are still talking around the fire.

I take another look around the cave. Surprisingly, there's not a ton of dirt in here. There's enough that it's not as if someone's been keeping it clean, but it's not gross. The entrance is mostly covered by debris. Some of it arranged there by Jay and Mitch, other stuff was just there when we got here. We have a small fire going by the entrance for some warmth and light. Kendra is now organizing all of our supplies against the wall of the cave.

"Tristan, are you glad we left?"

He looks me in the eye. "I'm glad that we're not in their hands. But I miss the safety, and the food, and not having this constant worry about staying alive."

"But you're not regretting your decision to choose me over Daniel and Oliver and all of them?"

"No Amber. Not one bit. I care about you so much."

"Are you gonna go back to B. C. when we're safe? Back to your family?"

"I have nothing in British Columbia," he replies curtly.

"But your family," I insist. "They must be missing-"

He stops me. "Amber. I promise you. I'm not missing anyone. You know what happens to street kids? The ADCCG takes us no matter what-"

"Tristan, I-I'm so sorry."

"No need Amber. A family is supposed to love you unconditionally. Family is with you forever. The love from your family is supposed to be infinite. I didn't get that from my family. Family is not defined by blood. I want to be with people I love more than anything else. I want to spend my life with people who love me just as much as I love them."

After a pause, I ask, "Then what are you going to do when we're safe?"

"Well, if you'll let me, I'd like to stay with you."

I wake up to voices and the crackling of a fire.

I sit up and blink a few times, adjusting to the light.

"Morning Amber," Kendra says cheerily.

"Hey guys."

"How's your ankle? Can I take a look?" Greyson asks.

"Its sore. Go ahead."

I take off the brace I got from the ADCCG, take off my sock, and roll up my pant leg.

"Jeez Amber. It's pretty swollen." He pauses. "But it's actually not quite as bad as I thought it would be. Need a pain pill?"

I laugh, but I'm annoyed. How dare he tease me about needing a pain pill that I can't get.

"You're so funny. Of course I do. But where are you going to get a pain pill? You gonna pull it out from behind my ear or something?"

Kendra laughs, but starts digging through our stuff. Moments later, she triumphantly chucks a rattling pill bottle to Greyson.

"Seriously?" I exclaim. I'm so happy! "How did you get these?"

"Got 'em from the infirmary a while ago," Jay tells me nonchalantly. "We knew you'd need them."

"Thank you so much!"

Greyson gives me a pill and one of our precious water bottles.

"Try not to drink too much of it," he warns me.

I swallow the pill. "What other magical goodies do we have that I don't know about?" I ask.

"Well," Tristan says, coming over from where him and Mitch were doing something at the little fire. "You have me, and I like to think that I'm pretty magical."

I laugh, and slap him jokingly. "Yeah, sure."

"But, really, let's go find out. Kendra sorted it all, but I fell asleep a couple minutes after you last night, so I don't know what we have."

"Hey Kendra? Can you show us what kinda stuff we have over there?"

"Yeah, of course."

Turns out we have a pretty decent amount of stuff. It's a lot more than I expected.

Kendra left our clothes in our bags so that they don't get all mixed up. I also notice that there's more than just clothes in Greyson and Jay's backpacks. It's probably stuff that's more valuable, or stuff we don't need right now. We have an assortment of protein bars and trail mix packets, some water bottles, blankets, a pack of matches, a two pocket knives, the rope ladder, the thing Greyson unlocked the door of the complex with, and a few other assorted things.

The fire is burning down now, but it's okay, because the sun is out now, and it's pretty warm.

"Guys, Mitch and I are gonna go walk around, see if there are any berries we can eat. Okay?"

"Alright," Jay says.

"Be safe guys," I say.

Mitch and Kendra have only been gone for twenty minutes or so when they come running back into our cave.

"Guys! Guys, guys guys, there's-there' people outside!" Kendra explains in a frantic whisper. "We came running back as soon as we heard them."

"Put everything in the bags! Hide in the back!" Greyson orders.

Tristan stomps the remains of our fire into nothing. Kendra, Mitch and I frantically pack everything up, and Jay and Greyson add a bit more to our 'barricade' at the door.

Then we all crawl back into the dark depths of the cave.

"You okay?" Tristan whispers into my ear.

"Yeah. Just scared."

He protectively wraps his arm around me.

We hear voices go by the entrance to our cave.

"Are you sure you disguised the entrance enough?" Kendra asks faintly.

"Shh. But yes, I'm certain," Greyson whispers.

We wait in silent darkness for what seems like hours. We can hear voices, and the static of radio communication.

"Search party to ADCCG. No news on the escapees yet. Over."

I can't believe it. How do they know we're gone? How can they find us so quickly? There are many different directions we could have gone.

"What are the approximate coordinates? Over." The man asks the person on the other line.

"You are right in the centre of the range the tracker is giving us. Over," is the reply.

"Control, remind me of exactly what the tracker is. Over."

"Lieutenant, the tracker is located in an ADCCG ankle brace one of the escapees was wearing. Please keep looking in every corner of the range the tracker gives. We can't afford the loss."

I'm sorry I went so long without an update! But I think I'm back now.

The song up at the top is Unconditionally by Katy Perry. Let me know if you can get sound when you're reading on your phone. I was struggling to make that thing work. That song was my inspiration for the Amber/Tristan scene.

I know you don't want to hear my excuses for not updating in over a month. All I'll say is that in the past month, I wrote two really crappy versions of this chapter, that I would have been embarrassed to post. But I'm very happy with the way this turned out.

Thanks for being awesome readers!

Jen

+24+

The ankle brace. Ohmygosh. Of course they put a tracker in it!

The search party slowly moves away and after what feels like days of siting in the same positions, getting stiffer and stiffer, we decide it's safe to move around and talk.

"No fire guys," Jay says. "We can't take the risk."

Greyson nods. "I made a plan while we were sitting."

Kendra eagerly urges him on. "We sure need one. Tell us."

"We should rest for a while and get ready. I want to take a look at the brace and see if we can remove the tracker. Then I'll take the tracker, or the whole brace and ditch it somewhere."

"You're going alone?" I ask.

"Yeah. It's safer."

What if they catch him? I only just found him, I can't bear to loose my big brother again.

"Are you sure?" Kendra asks, her tone reflecting my concern.

"As much as I hate to say it, he's right," Jay says and Mitch nods in agreement. The decision is made. Greyson will go alone.

"It'll be okay Amber," Tristan whispers in my ear. "You know how he is. He'll stay safe."

I nod, blinking back tears and trying to believe Tristan's words.

I need my big brother.

"Hey Amber? Can you pass us your brace?"

"Yep."

I undo the Velcro and toss it to the guys. My ankle is really stiff from staying still for so long, but I think it is feeling a bit better.

"It's less swollen," Tristan comments.

"Yeah. It's really stiff though."

"That's cause we crammed into the back of a cave together. I'm stiff too."

"Good. I'm glad I'm not the only one suffering."

"Your level of empathy never ceases to amaze me," he says with a laugh.

I smack him in the shoulder.

"Ow!"

"Oh hush, you big baby."

"Yeah well, you're stuck with me." He puts his arm around me in a peace offering.

Or so I thought.

Tristan starts tickling me. I try my hardest not to scream. I squirm around on the floor.

"Stop," I plead. "Truce!"

"Say Tristan is the greatest."

"Tristan is the greatest!"

2056

He lets me go. "Why thank you Amber. I'm glad you think I'm the greatest."

"Hey lovebirds!" Mitch calls, causing me to cringe. "Wanna come over here for a sec?"

"Okay."

"So we've looks at the brace, and there's no evidence of a tracker in it. So I'm going to have to take the whole brace with me," Greyson explains.

I nod. I still don't want him to go.

"We can use part of a blanket to wrap up your ankle Amber," Kendra tells me. "You need something to support it."

I nod again. "Greyson? Are you sure it's safe for you to go alone?"

"Amber, I promise you I will be super careful. It's safer for me to go by myself. Okay?"

His words are reassuring, but I'm still worried.

+++

The sun is going down, and it's time for Greyson to head out.

"Pack up everything while I'm gone. I think we should go somewhere else once I'm back."

Yes! Let's get far away from the ADCCG lieutenant.

Greyson stands up with the brace, whispers something to Tristan, and crawls through the entrance to the cave.

"Stay safe big brother."

"See you guys soon."

With Greyson gone, we aren't really sure what to do. We just sit around quietly until Kendra breaks the silence.

"Okay guys. We need to do something. Amber, come here. We'll make you a brace. Guys, start packing stuff up."

After a few attempts and some help from Mitch, Kendra has a strip of blanket ripped off. She carefully wraps it around my ankle in the same way the tensor bandage was wrapped in the ADCCG infirmary.

Then we go join Tristan, Jay and Mitch in packing up, and we finish pretty quickly.

+++

Passing time is scary. It gives me time alone with the worry that is consuming me, the thoughts and memories that haunt me. What if Greyson gets caught? Or we all get caught?

"Why am I so tired?" Kendra asks frustratedly. "All we've don is sit in this stupid cave!"

I know exactly what she means though. I've been fighting off this drowsy feeling for a while. But we haven't done anything to make us tired lately. Greyson is the one doing that.

"We may as well get some rest now," Jay says. "If we're gonna leave this place, we might as well be ready. Plus, we already packed up all our stuff.

"That sounds like a great idea," Kendra says.

"I'll keep watch for now," Mitch volunteers. "I'm not tired."

Jay nods and says, "If you want to keep watch then go ahead. I'd much rather sleep."

Mitch laughs and we pass around some blankets. I wrap myself in the blanket and get comfortable. It doesn't take long to fall asleep.

+++

"Amber."

"Amber, wake up."

Tristan wakes me up nicely. He doesn't jump on me like Ty would've, or pour water on me like Mitch once did to Tasha and I.

"Greyson has news," Tristan informs me.

I sit up abruptly. Greyson's back?

"What's the news?" I ask hurriedly.

"Just a minute. I'll tell you once Kendra's awake," Greyson tells me.

"You mean I'm not the last one to wake up?"

Greyson laughs. "For once!"

I go to my brother and hug him. "I was worried," I whisper.

"No need, baby sis. I'm safe."

"So Grey, how'd it go?" Kendra asks.

"Well," he starts, keeping us in suspense.

"Dude! Just tell us!" Jay protests.

"Okay, okay. I got rid of the ankle brace. Mission accomplished." We all interrupt him with soft applause. "But there's more."

"Did you find a million dollars?" Mitch asks.

"Or maybe our location?" Kendra says, slapping Mitch upside the head. "Cause six lost teenagers with a million dollars wouldn't look suspicious at all."

"Neither," Greyson tells us.

"Then what did you find?" Tristan asks.

"I'll tell you. I was walking in the direction we came, with the ADCCG behind me. South. I wanted to go really far away, but still make it look like we were on the run. But then I found a town-"

"A town?" I ask curiously.

"Yeah. So I went way east of the town and left the tracker and then came back here."

"So there's a town," Kendra speculates. "We're close to people."

+++

Hi guys! What do you think? What do you think they are going to do?

Vote and comment please! I love every one of you guys that take the time to read my book. But if you're being a ghost reader, then I don't know that you're reading my book. But thank you to everyone who is supporting me as I write this book!

Jen

-25-

We've finally reached a decision. Actually no. It's a compromise. Kendra, Jay and Tristan were certain we should go to the town. Mitch and Greyson we dead set against it. And me, well, I'm somewhere in the middle.

But the final decision is that we will walk towards the town, and find somewhere in the nearby woods to stay for the time being. We all want to be out of this area that the people were searching for us.

We're ready to go. We can continue on our escape now. I don't really care where we go, I'm just happy that we're walking away from the ADCCG complex.

"Everyone have their backpack?" Jay asks.

We all confirm that yes, we have everything.

"Amber, how's your ankle?" Kendra asks me. "Need to rewrap it?"

"Uhh..."

"I'm gonna take that as a yes."

I roll up my pant leg. "Yeah, it's definitely not doing much right now. We need to have your ankle wrapped tighter if you want it to be supported," Kendra tells me, and expertly wraps the bandage.

"You're really good at that," I tell her.

She smiles modestly and says, "I always wanted to be a doctor. The ADCCG stole that dream from me."

Mitch puts his arm around her. "But we're out now, love."

"We're not out of the woods yet guys."

I groan. "Greyson, why? Why do you torture us with your horrible puns?"

Tristan laughs. "Oh come on. It was pretty good."

"No it wasn't. You deserve to be slapped for saying that," I tell him, and of course, slap him.

"You know you love me."

"Come on you guys. Let's go," Jay urges. The sun is setting, and it's time for our departure.

Greyson leads, since he's the only one who knows where we're going. Jay is beside him, Tristan and I behind, and Mitch and Kendra are bring up the rear.

"So," Tristan says. "Are you still undecided?"

"Yeah. I really don't know. Like-I'm scared that if we go into the town we'll get caught, because we would be suspicious looking. But staying in the forest, we'll never know exactly where we are, and we're gonna run out of food eventually. There's good and bad for both, and I just can't decide which option I like better." I stop. Another reason is that I would like to see my family, but I don't know if I should say it, with what I know about Tristan's family.

"You want to go home eventually, don't you?" He asks me, thinking one step ahead of me, like always.

"Yeah," I mutter.

"Amber, it's fine. I'm used to it by now. I don't want to go back to my family. But maybe someday I'll meet yours."

"Well you've already met Greyson," I say with a smile.

"I think he hates me."

I laugh. "Nah, I think he just decided to play the role of the over-protective brother."

Tristan laughs.

We walk in silence for awhile. One of my favourite things about being with Tristan is that we don't need to always be talking. There's no pressure to fill the silence with him.

I'm mulling this over when I feel a drop of rain hit my forehead.

"Did you feel that?" I ask.

"Feel what?" Tristan asks me.

"Rain. A rain drop just fell on my face."

"I think you're going crazy Amber. There's no rain."

"I swear, I felt rain."

We continue walking, no one else feels the rain.

"Wait, guys!" Mitch calls out. "Amber was right! I felt a raindrop too!"

Soon enough, we're all feeling the light rain on our heads. We've been pretty lucky with weather so far, so we can't really complain about a little rain.

I've always liked rain. The smell, the feeling on your hair, the raindrops on plants. Rain-the symbol of new beginnings. A dirty slate wiped clean. We will move on. Aria will always stay with me in my mind. I'll never forget how she was always willing to talk in the bathroom, even if I was too stupid and chose my other "friends" over her.

"Whatcha thinking about Amber?" Tristan asks me.

"The rain. It lead me to thinking about Aria."

He pulls an arm around me. I don't need to hear words to tell that he cares about me. This simple gesture is more that enough.

"Do you ever miss them?" I ask. "Your family?"

He looks down at the ground and doesn't say anything. Crap. Why did I even ask.

"Sorry. I-I shouldn't have asked."

"No-no, sorry Amber. It's fine. It just made me think." I return his previous gesture and squeeze his hand. "I had a little sister. When my parents left us alone, I tried Amber. I tried really hard. All I wanted was for her to be safe. But when they took me-"

"The government?" I ask.

He nods. "When they took me I had to leave her. She was nine. Five years younger than me. I'm sure they found her and took her too."

"What was her name?"

"Marissa," he whispers.

We walk in silence, hand in hand.

We arrive at clearing, and Greyson points at where the town is. It's just a bit down the hill. This will be a good place to stay for a bit.

"I don't think we should risk a fire," I say. "People will see."

"Yeah. And it's not too cold," Mitch agrees.

"What do we have for food?" Asks Kendra. "I'm hungry."

"I have an unopened pack of dried fruit in my bag," Greyson tells us. "Let's have that."

We sit down in a circle and pass around the bag of dried fruit. It might not seem like much, but we haven't had a lot to eat lately, so any food is good.

"Kendra, can you come help me wrap my ankle?"

"Yeah, of course."

"How do you do that so well?" Tristan asks.

"Just something I'm good at I guess," she tells him. "I've learned some tricks along the way."

My ankle feels a lot better with the added support.

"Thanks Kendra."

"Who do you think lives in the town?" Asks Mitch.

"Random people, probably," Greyson says, ever the practical one.

"Maybe they're witches and wizards," Jay guesses.

"Or what if it's a ghost town."

"Or maybe it's a bunch of criminals, removed from society."

"Or a group of illegal immigrants."

"You guys are crazy," I say. They continue making up their crazy theories though.

"They're crazy," Greyson says, "but we love them all the same." And he's right.

We spend the night camped out with blankets, and backpacks and hoodies as pillows under the stars.

As much as I hate it, because it's so, so cheesy, having Tristan beside me makes me feel safe.

Being under the stars makes me think of all the evenings Tasha and I spent on the balcony at her house; spending hours talking, laughing and living life. I miss her.

I hear Tristan roll over beside me.

"Are you awake?" I whisper. I had assumed everyone else was already asleep.

"Yeah. I didn't realize you were still awake."

I sit up a bit and prop myself up on my elbow.

"How's your ankle?" He asks me.

"Not hurting. I rewrapped it a little while ago."

"That's good."

Tristan goes quiet. There must be something on his mind.

"Tristan?" I ask, at the same time he says "Amber?"

"Sorry, go ahead," he tells me.

"No, I was just going to ask what you were thinking about," I tell him.

"Well, honestly, I was thinking about you." He stops. "I haven't had the balls to say this sooner, and maybe this isn't the time to ask, considering the fact that we're like, running away from a corrupt government and stuff, but I just have to ask you. Do you want to be my girlfriend, Amber?"

"Only if you want to be my boyfriend," I say with a smile.

He laughs at my smart aleck comment. "Of course."

I want to tell someone. I want to talk to Aria, or Tasha, or even my mom. But I can't talk to anyone. They're not here.

"Do you think I'll ever see my family again?"

"I don't know Amber. But I hope so."

"I hope so too. I miss them." Then I have an idea. "Tristan, will you tell me a story?" I ask.

"About what? I don't have any stories."

"Anything. I want a story."

"Well, once upon a time, there was a beautiful girl named Amber-"

"Not like that, dummy. Tell me a story that happened to you," I say.

"Okay, okay," he says laughing. "Um," he pauses to think. "Oh! When I was in grade three, my class took a field trip to the zoo. My best friend at the time, Will, well, he wasn't the smartest kid. I spent the whole bus ride to the zoo convincing him that there world be unicorns there. I had never been to the zoo either-both of us came from rough families-but I knew well enough that there wouldn't be unicorns."

I laugh. Little Tristan must have been so cute.

"So when we got to the zoo, Will runs straight to where the teacher is talking with the tour guide. And he's jumping up and down and shouting that he wants to see the unicorns first, and then everyone else got all excited and wanted to see the unicorns. It was my greatest elementary school moment."

"Who knew that eight year old Tristan was such a master mind?" I ask with a laugh.

Tristan joins my quiet laughter. I roll onto my back and look at the stars.

"It's so pretty out here. I never got that in the city," I say.

"It is. I always wanted to go camping. My parents didn't really care about what we wanted though."

I give his hand a squeeze. Eventually we fall asleep like that. Hand in hand, faces to the sky.

Hey guys! I'm really sorry that you had to wait so long for this chapter! But the next chapter is already close ish to done.

Sadly, this is the second last chapter in the book (unless I decide I can't part with this story and write another chapter!). So I should have chapter 26 up soon.

Thanks so much for reading, voting and commenting-it means so much to me!!

Jen

+26+

"C'mon sleepyheads, get up!"

I sit up and look around. Jay is the only one up, the rest of us are rubbing our eyes groggily.

"Seriously Jay?" Kendra asks. "It wouldn't have killed us to get some extra sleep."

"Yeah, yeah, yeah. But we have to do something about our food situation. Right now each of us get half a protein bar, and then we have no food."

Thinking of food reminds me of the ache in my stomach. We've been rationing the food, but we didn't have that much to begin with.

"Crap," Mitch mutters.

"We might as well eat the last of our food then. I think I speak for all of us when I say that I'm hungry," Tristan says.

"Yeah. I guess it just makes the decision about going into the town," Greyson says, surprising us all, because he really didn't want to go.

Jay passes a protein bar to Kendra and me, and keeps one for him and Greyson.

"Don't even think about giving me a bigger piece cause I eat more," Tristan warns me.

"I would've, if I wasn't so hungry," I say, breaking the bar in half.

After eating the last of our food, we pack everything into our backpacks.

I can't believe it. We're going into a town. It's so exciting, but terrifying. What if they send us right back to the complex. Or worse, what if they kill us on the spot?

Just as we're about to leave the clearing, we hear a small voice say, "Who are you?"

Looking around, I see a small girl who can't be more than ten. She has brown hair tied up in pigtails and is wearing brown pants and a blue shirt. Her clothes look to be very worn out.

"Are you lost?" She asks.

Kendra bends down to talk to her. "Not exactly. Who are you?" She asks in a kind voice.

"I'm Elaina," she tells us. "I live over there," she says, gesturing to where the town is. "Daddy taught me that I have to bring lost people to him. Come on."

I'm skeptical to take orders from a little girl, but what else can we do? We were going to go into the town anyway.

It's about a five minute walk down a hill and into the town. I stumbled twice because of my ankle, and Tristan-my boyfriend, I think with a smile-caught me both times.

Elaina leads us into the town, and straight to a small house. The whole town seems to be pretty old looking, but it's really cute.

"Daddy!" She calls. "I found lost people!"

A man, who I assume to be her father, comes to the front door. He seems very surprised to see us.

"I'm going to take them to the centre square, Elaina. Please go get Mr Browley and Mr and Mrs Calder."

Elaina nods and runs off. Her father leads us to the centre square quietly.

"It's been a long time since we got visitors like y'all. We're gonna hafta decide what we're gonna do with y'all. Where are ya kids from?"

"We ran away sir," Greyson tells him, giving away as little information as possible.

The man doesn't seem happy with the minimal information, but he hasn't told us anything either.

Elaina returns with three adults. A man who looks to be about mid thirties, like Elaina's father, and an older man and woman.

As the four adults talk to Elaina, townspeople gather around the square.

The man who I assume is Mr Browley claps his hands and gets the attention of the crowd.

"As y'all can see, we have here six young people here in the centre of town. Little Elaina found these six camped out in the woods. We're gonna figure out where they came from, and decide what to do with them shortly. We need two other council members to come and help us."

A man and a woman step forward, and everyone else in the crowd disperses.

Elaina's father tells us that they are going to question each of us separately to see if we tell the truth. Then they'll decide what they're doing with us.

"If all of y'alls stories don't match up, there's gonna be trouble," he warns.

Tell the truth, Greyson mouths to us.

They take each of us different ways. I luck out, and am with the older lady. I'm very glad, because the men were a lot more intimidating.

"What's your name sugar?" The lady asks me as she leads me away from the square.

"I'm Amber," I tell her.

"Well Amber, I'm Mrs Calder," she tells me. "Oh dear! Did you injure yourself?" She asks, noticing my limp.

"Yes, awhile back," I tell her.

We reach a house, and she opens the door for me. "Take a seat honey," she says, motioning at the kitchen table.

"Would you like anything?" She asks. "Some tea? Or if you're hungry, I have fresh bannock and jam."

"Could I have some bannock please?"

"Jam too?"

"Yes please."

Mrs Calder places a plate of bannock and strawberry jam in front of me. The smell reminds me of cooking it over the fire with my neighbours.

"So Amber, what's your story?" Mrs Calder asks.

"The six of us were ADCCG kids. We escaped."

"Oh. Who are the others you are with?"

"Kendra is the other girl. Then there's Greyson, who is my brother, Mitch, who is also from my province, Jay and Tristan. There's not really much to the story. There were two others with us, but they didn't make it," I say sadly.

"Oh dear. Well, you stay here and eat. Feel free to take more bannock, I'm sure you're hungry. I have to report to the others. I'll be back soon Amber."

Mrs Calder heads back to the town square. After I finish my bannock, I look around. The kitchen is simple, and there are no modern appliances. There is a wood stove, and the jam is in a metal ice box. It's like stepping into the past.

I sit in the kitchen for a long time. I want to check out the rest of the house, but I don't want to be rude. Instead, I take another piece of bannock.

Mrs Calder returns and tells me that we are going back to the town square.

I clasp my hands worriedly. What if someone missed Greyson's message and tried to make up a cover story? What would they do to us?

"Don't worry, honey," Mrs Calder assures me.

Mrs Calder and I are the last to arrive at the town square.

After debriefing quickly, the adults turn to us.

"Your stories matched up," one of the men tells us. "We've decided that if you would like, we will allow you to stay in our little village,

Johnston. Our village is special. We are all here, hiding from the government. No one has any idea that this village exists. We live a simple life, with out electricity. But we are safe here. It's a good life. Take some time to decide."

Kendra jumps into Mitch's arms, and Tristan picks me up and spins me around. I notice Jay and Greyson standing around awkwardly.

"One second," I tell Tristan.

I run to Greyson and jump on him, giving him a big hug.

"We did it! We're safe!" I exclaim.

After our celebration, we go back toning serious, and I ask the question we all have on our minds.

"Are we going to stay?"

"What do you guys think?" Jay asks.

"I think we should stay," I say. Mrs Calder was so nice and welcoming.

"Stay," Tristan agrees.

"Stay," says Kendra, looking expectantly at Mitch.

"As much as it surprises me to say it, I think we should stay."

"I'm all for staying," Jay says. "What about you, Greyson?"

"Let's stay."

Final chapter! Don't cry Jen, don't cry. There will be an epilogue soon though!

Thanks so much for reading! Vote and comment please!

Jen

Epilogue

Everybody has to make choices. And sometimes those choices cause you to lose important things.

The day I chose to pass my ADCCG fitness exam, I made a choice. I knew that being taken would result in my life drastically changing. I knew that I would be leaving my family and friends behind.

I had to go though. My life has changed, but I've learned so much! Sure, I never really found out exactly why the ADCCG exists, but maybe one day I will.

But I did get to meet my big brother, who I otherwise never would have met. I became friends with Aria, and learned so much from her. She taught me how we hold ourselves higher than others, and choose not to see some people. I met Tristan, who has changed my life for good.

Leaving and staying. Choices I've had to make. There are days when I regret leaving Winnipeg. I have days when I think that maybe we shouldn't have stayed here in Johnston.

I miss the people I left behind, but I never would have me the amazing 'family' I have here, had I stayed.

And since that day three weeks ago, when Tristan asked me to be his wife, I've known that I made the right choices.

I remember that day as well as I remember the same day ten years earlier. The day we came to Johnston.

After deciding to stay, Mrs Calder gave me a hug. "Welcome to Johnston," she said.

I smiled. "Thank you."

Mrs Calder then suggested to the man I assumed to be Mr Calder that we all go over to their house and have some bannock with jam and tea.

The six of us, and the six village council members sat down in the Calder's kitchen. Mrs Calder set plates of bannock in front of us. Even though she had already fed me, I ate as quickly as the others.

I remember Kendra apologizing for our awful manners. "We haven't had much food lately," she said.

They set out what was going to happen. There weren't any extra places for us to call our own, so for the first year Kendra and I stayed with the Calder's, Tristan and Mitch stayed with an older man who lives on his own, and Jay and Greyson stayed with Elaina and her dad.

They told us we would have to build our own places, but promised that there would be lots of help from everyone else, provided that we pull our weight in the community.

"We don't have electricity," they told us. "We cook on wood stoves, do our laundry by hand, keep ice in metal iceboxes to keep our food cold. Electricity would make it easier to find us."

It was all really overwhelming back then. Now it just seems normal.

The first year took a lot of adjusting. But eventually we all had a place to live. Kendra and Mitch moved into one of the new little houses together. Greyson and I moved into one, and Jay and Tristan were left with the other.

Nowadays we all have our own jobs. Kendra works with a lady named Sarah as the village doctors. Greyson, Jay and Mitch help with construction and other miscellaneous jobs like that. Tristan works in the field, helping with the vegetables we grow. And I help look after the kids during the day.

Everyone has to make tough choices. Some people look back with regrets. But I am happy with the choices I've made.

---END---